"This is a marriage of convenience, yes?"

"Marriages of convenience don't produce children. I need children." Before she could speak he continued. "I'll do my best to ensure you're satisfied. I want you to be happy. It's important we're both fulfilled. Sex is a natural part of life. It should be natural between us."

Blood surged to her face, heating her cheeks, creating a frisson of warmth through her limbs. "We hardly know each other, Mr. Pateras."

"Which is why I won't force myself on you. I'm content to wait until some of the newness wears off and we've grown more...comfortable with each other before becoming intimate."

Jane Porter

CHRISTOS'S PROMISE

Passion™

TORONTO • NEW YORK • LONDON
AMSTERDAM • PARIS • SYDNEY • HAMBURG
STOCKHOLM • ATHENS • TOKYO • MILAN • MADRID
PRAGUE • WARSAW • BUDAPEST • AUCKLAND

For my husband, Joe. You are my miracle.

ISBN 0-373-12210-1

CHRISTOS'S PROMISE

First North American Publication 2001.

Copyright © 2001 by Jane Porter.

CHAPTER ONE

"YOU'D rather remain locked here in the convent than marry me?"

Disbelief echoed in Christos Pateras's voice. How could this girl—woman, actually, although she didn't look a bit like the twenty-five her father claimed she was—prefer living in the spartan convent over marrying him?

He was no barbarian. Compared to the Greek men she'd been raised with, he was downright civilized.

"You had my answer earlier," Alysia Lemos retorted coolly. "You needn't have wasted your time coming here."

He turned his back on the anxious nun hovering in the background, intentionally making it harder for her to hear. The abbess might have insisted on providing Alysia with a chaperone, but that didn't mean the sister needed to be privy to the conversation.

"You told your father no," Christos answered, his tone mild, deceptively so. "You didn't tell *me* no." He rarely raised his voice. He didn't need to. His size and authority generally were persuasive enough.

But Alysia Lemos's fine dark eyebrows only arched higher. "Some women might find such persistence flattering. I don't."

"So, your answer is…?"

5

Alysia's incredulous laughter contrasted sharply with the dark blaze in her eyes. "I know you're an American, but surely you can't be this much of an idiot!"

Her cutting dismissal might have crushed a man of lesser ego, but he wasn't just any man, and Miss Lemos wasn't just any woman. He needed her. He wasn't going to leave Oinoussai without her. "You dislike Americans?"

"Not all."

"Good. That should help ease the transition when we move to New York."

Her eyes met his, the dark irises all the more arresting against her sudden pallor. "I'm not moving. And I'd never agree to an arranged marriage."

He dismissed this along with her other protestations. "In case you're worried, I consider myself Greek. My parents were born here, on Oinoussai. They still call this home."

"Oh, happy people, they."

He almost smiled. No wonder her father, Darius, was feeling desperate. She was not an eager bride-to-be. "I don't know if they'll be happy with you for a daughter-in-law, but they'll adjust."

Bands of color burned along the curve of her cheek. "I'm sure your mother dotes on you."

"Endlessly. But then, most Greek mothers live for their sons."

"While daughters are disposable."

He gave no indication that he'd heard the hurt in her voice, the small wobble in her breath as she spat the bitter words. "Not mine. My daughters will be cherished."

At thirty-seven, he needed a wife, and Darius Lemos needed a husband for his wayward daughter. This was no love match, but a match made in a bank in Switzerland. "I'm an only child, the last of the Pateras in my branch of the family. I've promised my parents a grandchild before my thirty-ninth birthday, and I shall deliver."

"No, you hope *I'll* deliver!"

He bit the inside of his cheek to keep from smiling. "I stand corrected."

Alysia's hands balled. She longed to smack his smirk right off his gorgeous, arrogant face. She'd never met a man more sure of himself than he. Except for her father, that is.

She swallowed convulsively, her stomach heaving, as she struggled to understand why her father had reached across the Atlantic for a husband for her. Her father despised the new rich. Her father must be feeling desperate. Well, so was she. He was practically auctioning her off to the highest bidder, his sole heir up for grabs.

Hot tears rushed to her eyes but she held them back. Her mother would never have let her father do this.

"There are worse bridegrooms, Miss Lemos."

She felt the irony but couldn't even smile. "A husband is a husband, and I don't want one."

"Most women want to be married. It's the desire of every Greek woman."

"I'm not most women."

He laughed almost unkindly. "So say you, but I've learned one woman is not so different from another. You all have agendas—"

"And you don't?"

"Mine isn't hidden. I want children. I need children." He scrutinized her as though she were horseflesh. "You're young. You'd be an excellent mother."

She winced. "I don't want to be a mother."

He shrugged, unconcerned. "We can marry today. Here. It'll just be us. Your father is unavailable, I'm afraid."

"What a shame."

His mouth quirked faintly, revealing surprise, even intrigue. "You speak like a sailor."

"The closest I've come to my father's business."

"You're interested in business?"

"I'm interested in my competition." The industry her father loved above all else. Nothing came between him and his ships. Nothing had ever been allowed to interfere with the great Lemos fortune. Not her mother. Certainly not herself.

"I think the business would bore you," he said after a moment, jamming his hands into trouser pockets. "It's talks. Contracts. Number crunching. Tedious stuff."

"For my small brain?"

His eyes glimmered, her mocking tone had made him smile. "You shouldn't listen to everything your father says," he cheerfully drawled. "Only the good things about me."

She could easily have slapped his cheeky face. She knew exactly why Christos Pateras was marrying her. He wanted her dowry. Her dowry and her father's shipping interests. When Darius passed away, Christos would inherit Lemos's empire. "You're overly confident."

"So say my critics."

"You have many?"

"Legions."

She offered him her profile, grinding her teeth together. This was a joke to him and he toyed with her like a cat with a mouse. She struggled to contain her temper, her smooth jaw tightening. "You're mad if you think I'll marry you."

"Your father has already consented to the marriage. The dowry has changed hands—"

"Change it back!"

"Can't do that. I need you too much."

She turned her head, her brilliant gaze catching his. "Despite what you both think, I am neither mindless, nor spineless. Since you appear to have difficulty with your hearing, let me say it again. I will not marry you, Mr. Pateras. I will never marry you, Mr. Pateras. I'd rather grow old and gray in this convent than take your name, Mr. Pateras."

Christos rocked back on his heels and fought his desire to smile. Her father said she was difficult but he hadn't mentioned his daughter's intelligence, or spirit. There was a difference between difficult and spirited. Difficult was unpleasant. Spirited was something a man quite enjoyed. Like a spirited horse, a spirited chase, a spirited game of tennis. But nothing was more appealing than a spirited woman. "Oh, I think I quite like you," he murmured softly.

"The feeling isn't mutual."

His lips curved, and he watched as she threw her head back, dark eyes challenging him.

With the sunlight washing her face, he suddenly realized her eyes weren't brown at all, but blue. A mysterious, dark blue. Like the sky at night. Like the Aegean Sea before a storm. Honey wheat hair and Aegean eyes. She looked remarkably like the pictures he'd seen of her half-English, half-Greek mother, a woman considered to be one of the great beauties of her time.

"Hopefully you'll grow to tolerate me. It'd make conjugal life…bearable."

A pulse beat wildly at the base of her throat. But her eyes splintered anger, passion, denial. She was going to fight him, tooth and nail. "I'd sooner let you put a bit in my mouth and saddle on my back."

"Now that could be tempting."

Her cheeks darkened to a dusky pink, her gorgeous coloring a result of the Greek-English heritage. Blue eyes, sun-streaked hair, a hint of gold in her complexion. He felt desire, and possession. She was his. She just didn't know it yet.

Alysia fled to a distant corner of the walled garden, arms crossed over her chest, breasts rising and falling with her quick, shallow breathing.

He followed more slowly, not wanting to push her too hard. At least not yet. Furtively he touched the breast pocket of his coat, feeling the crisp edges of the morning's newspaper. She wouldn't like the press clipping. He was the first to admit it was a power play, and underhanded, but Christos wasn't about to lose this deal.

He'd made a promise to his parents that he'd bring fortune to his beleaguered branch of the family, and every decision he'd made since then had been in the pursuit of that goal. Since he'd made that promise, the family fortunes had grown into a different league. Very different.

She must have felt him approach. "Have you no ethics?" Her low-pitched voice vibrated with emotion. "How can you marry a woman against her will?"

"It wouldn't be against your will. You have a choice."

"You disgust me!"

"Then go back inside. Call the nun over. She's dying to be part of the conversation."

Alysia glanced over her shoulder, spotted the nun and pressed her lips together. "You're enjoying this."

"It's my wedding day. What's not to enjoy?"

She took another step away, sinking onto a polished marble bench. He walked around the bench to face her. "Alysia, your father has sworn to leave you here until we exchange vows. Doesn't that worry you?"

"No. You are not the first man I've refused, and dare I say, nor the last. I've been here nearly a year, and the sisters have been wonderful. Quite frankly, I've begun to think of the convent as home."

The convent as home? He didn't believe her, not for a minute. Despite her refined beauty—the high, fine cheekbones, the elegant curve of her brow—her eyes, those indigo-blue eyes, smoldered with secrets.

She did not belong in the convent's simple brown smock any more than he belonged in priestly robes. And God knew he did not belong in priestly robes.

Christos felt a sudden wave of sympathy for her, but not enough to walk away from the playing table. No, he never walked away from the playing table, not that he played cards. He gambled in other ways. Daring, breathtaking power plays in the Greek shipping-industry which so far had resulted in staggering financial gain. He'd been wildly successful by anyone's standards.

"Your home, Alysia, will be with me. I've picked you. You are part of my plan. And once I put a plan into action, I don't give up. I never quit."

"Those admirable traits would be better applied elsewhere."

"There is no elsewhere. There is no other option. You, our marriage, is the future," he said softly, as a warm breeze blew through the courtyard, loosening a tendril of hair from her demure bun. She didn't attempt to smooth it and the golden-brown tendril floated light as a feather.

He liked the play of sunlight across her shoulders

and face. The sun turned her hair to gold and copper. Flecks of aquamarine shimmered in her eyes.

"I know who you are, Mr. Pateras. I'm not ignorant of your success." Her eyebrows arched. "Shall I tell you what I know?"

"Please. I enjoy my success story."

"A full-blooded Greek, you were born and raised in a middle-class New York suburb. You attended public school, before being accepted to one of the prestigious American Ivy League colleges."

"Yale," he supplied.

"Which is quite good," she agreed. "But why not Harvard? Harvard is supposed to be the best."

"Harvard is for old money."

"That's right. Your father left Oinoussai broke and in disgrace."

"Not disgraced. Just poor. Hopeful that there would be a better life elsewhere."

"Your father worked in the shipyards."

"He was a welder," Christos answered evenly, hiding the depth of his emotions. He was fiercely loyal to his parents, but particularly to his father. His father's piety, unwavering morals and devotion to family had sustained them during times of great financial hardship. And there had been hardship, tremendous hardship, not to mention ostracism in the close-knit Greek-American community.

Quickly, before she could probe further, he turned the spotlight on her. "And your father, Alysia, inherited his millions. You've never lacked for anything. You have no idea what 'poor' means."

"But you aren't poor anymore, Mr. Pateras. You now own as many ships as Britain's entire merchant fleet. Despite your humble origins, it shouldn't be difficult to find a bride a...trifle...more eager to accept your proposal."

"I can't find another Darius Lemos."

"So in reality you're marrying my father."

She was smart. He smiled faintly, again amused by the contradiction between her serene exterior and fiery interior. He found himself suddenly wondering what she'd be like in bed. Passionate as hell, probably.

He watched the shimmering golden-brown tendril dance across her cheek, caress her ear, and Christos felt a sudden urge to follow the tendril with his tongue, drawing the same tantalizing path from her cheekbone to her jaw, from her jaw to the hollow beneath her earlobe.

His body tightened, desire stirring. He'd enjoy being married to a woman like this. Procreation would be a pleasure.

Alysia leaned back on the bench, her brown shift outlining her small breasts, her dark lashes lowering to conceal her expression. "How well do you know my father?"

"Well enough to know what he is."

She allowed herself a small smile, and Christos noticed the flash of dimple to the left of her full mouth. He'd taste that, too, after the wedding.

"My father must be quite pleased to have you in his back pocket. I can quite picture him, rubbing his hands together, chuckling gleefully.'' Her head cocked, her lashes lifted, revealing the dark sapphire irises. "He did rub his hands after you made your deal, didn't he?''

Her tone, her voice, her eyes. He wanted her.

Abruptly he leaned forward, captured the coil of hair at her nape in his hand. Her eyes widened as his fingers tightened in her hair seconds before he covered her mouth with his.

Alysia inhaled as his lips touched hers, and he traced the soft outline of her lips with his tongue. He didn't miss her gasp, or the sudden softness in her mouth.

His own body hardened, blood surging. From the distance he heard a cough. The nun! Wouldn't do to get thrown out of here just yet.

Slowly he released her. "You taste beautiful.''

Alysia paled and dragged the back of her hand across her soft mouth, as if to rub away the imprint of his lips. "Try that again and I shall send for the abbess!''

He placed his foot on the bench, on the outside of her thigh. He felt the tremor in her body. "And say what, sweet Alysia? That your husband kissed you?''

"We are not married! We're not even engaged.''

"But soon shall be.'' He gazed at her exposed collarbone and the rise of fabric at her breasts. "Do you like wagers?''

She visibly shuddered. "No. I never gamble.''

"That's admirable. But I like bets, and I like these

odds. You see, Alysia, I know more about *you* than you think.''

He caught her incredulous expression, and felt a stab of satisfaction. ''You won an academic scholarship at seventeen to an art school in Paris. You lived in a garret with a dozen other want-to-be artists, a rather bohemian lifestyle with small children running underfoot. When money ran out, you, like the others, did odd jobs. One summer you worked as a housekeeper. You did a stint in a bakery. Your longest job was as a nanny for a designer and his family.''

''They were respectable jobs,'' she said faintly, blood draining from her face.

''Very respectable, but quite a change from life with a silver spoon in your mouth.''

''Is there a point to this?''

His smile faded and he leaned forward, trapping her between his knee and chest. ''You've spent eight years of your life trying to escape your father.''

Her lips parted but no sound came out.

He watched her closely, reading every flicker in her eyes. ''For a while, you were free. You painted, you traveled, you enjoyed an interesting circle of friends. But then you became ill, and your obliging father placed you in a hospital in Bern. Since then, he's owned you, body and soul.''

''Body, maybe, but not my soul. Never my soul!''

Again the fire, the spirited defiance. He felt a kinship with her that he felt with few women. He softened his tone, appealing to her intellect. ''Think about it, Alysia. In Greece you're powerless. Your father is the head of the household, the absolute authority. He has the right to choose your husband. He has the right to leave you locked up here. He has the right to make your life miserable.''

"I'm no prisoner here."

"Then why don't you leave?

She held her breath, exquisitely attentive, her eyes enormous, her lips compressed.

"Now, if I were your husband," he concluded after the briefest hesitation, "you could leave. Today. Right away. You'd finally be free."

She didn't speak for a moment, studying him with the same intentness with which she listened. After a moment she exhaled. "Greek wives are never free!''

"No, maybe not the way you think of it. But I'd permit you to travel, to pursue hobbies that interested you, to make friends of your own choosing.'' He shrugged. "You could even paint again."

"I don't paint anymore."

"But you could. I've heard you were quite good."

She suddenly laughed, her voice pitched low, her body nearly trembling with tension. She wrapped her arms across her chest, a makeshift cape, a protective embrace. "You must want my father's ships very much!"

Christos felt a wave of bittersweet emotion, unlike anything he'd ever felt before. He saw himself exactly as he was. Driven, calculating, proudly self-serving. And this woman, this lovely refined young woman, knew she mattered only in business terms.

Her worth was her name. Her value lay in her dowry. For a split second he hated the system and he hated himself and then he ruthlessly pushed his objection aside.

He would have her.

Alysia slipped from beneath his arm, taking several steps away. She walked to the edge of the herb garden and knelt at the flowering lavender. "Ships," she whispered, breaking off a purple stalk. "I hate them."

She carried the tuft of lavender to her nose, smelling it.

"And I love them," he answered, thinking she should have been a painting.

The bend of her neck, the creamy nape, the shimmering coil of hair the color of wild honey, the sun's golden caress.

He wanted this woman. Deal or no.

She crumpled the lavender stalk in her fist. "Mr. Pateras, has it crossed your mind to ask *why* a man as wealthy as my father must give away his fortune in order to get his daughter off his hands?"

The sunlight shone warm and gold on her head. The breeze loosened yet another shimmering tendril.

"I'm damaged goods, Mr. Pateras. My father couldn't give me away to a local Greek suitor, even if he tried."

More damaged than he'd ever know, Alysia acknowledged bleakly, clutching the broken lavender stalk in her palm. Unwillingly memories of the Swiss sanatorium came to mind. She'd spent nearly fourteen months there, all of her twenty-first year, before her mother came, rescuing her and helping her find a small flat in Geneva.

Alysia had liked Geneva. No bad memories there.

And for nearly two years she'd lived quietly, happily, content with her job in a small clothing shop, finding safety in her simple flat. Weekly she rang up her mother in Oinoussai and they chatted about inconsequential matters, the kind of conversation that doesn't challenge but soothes.

Her mother never discussed the sanatorium with her, nor Paris. Alysia never asked about her father. But they understood each other and knew the other's pain.

Alysia would never have returned to Greece, or her father's house, if it hadn't been for her mother's cancer.

The mournful toll of bells stirred Alysia, and she tensed, lashes lowering, mouth compressing, finding the bells an intolerable reminder of her mother's death and funeral.

The bells continued to ring, their tolling like nails scratching down a blackboard, sharp, grating. Oh, how she hated it here! The sisters had done everything they could to comfort her, and befriend her, but Alysia couldn't bear another day of bells and prayers and silence.

She didn't want to be reminded of her losses. She wanted to just get on with the living.

Sister Elena, a dour-faced nun with a heart of gold, signaled it was time to return inside.

Alysia felt a swell of panic, desperation making her light-headed. Suddenly she couldn't bear to leave the garden, or the promise of freedom.

As if sensing her reluctance, Christos extended a hand in her direction. "You don't have to go in. You could leave with me instead."

It was almost as if he could feel her weakening, sense her confusion. His tone gentled yet again. "Leave with me today and you'll have a fresh start, lead a different life. Everything would be exciting and new."

He was teasing her, toying with her, and she longed for the freedom even as she shrank from the bargain.

She could leave the convent if she went as his wife.

She could escape her father if she bound herself to this stranger.

"You're not afraid of me?" she asked, turning from Sister Elena's worried gaze to the darkly handsome American Greek standing just a foot away.

"Should I be?"

"I know my father must have mentioned my... health." She gritted against the sting of the words, each like a drop of poison on her tongue. Unwilling tears burned at the back of her eyes.

"He mentioned you hadn't been well a few years ago, but he assured me you're well now. And you look well. Quite well, if rather too thin, as a matter of fact."

Her lips curved into a small, cold self-mocking smile. "Looks can be deceiving."

Christos Pateras shrugged. "My first seven ships were damaged. I stripped them to the hull, refurbished each from bow to stern. Within a year my ships made me my first million. It's been ten years. They're still the workhorses of my fleet."

She envisioned him stripping her bare and attempting to make something of her. The vivid picture shocked and frightened her. It'd been years and years since she'd been intimate with a man, and this man, was nothing like her teenage lovers.

Hating the flush creeping through her cheeks, she lifted her chin. "I won't make you any millions."

"You already have."

Stung by his ruthless assessment, she tensed, her slender spine stiffening. "You'll have to give it back. I told you already, I shall never marry."

"*Again,* you mean. You'll never marry *again.*"

She froze where she stood, at the edge of the herb garden, her gaze fixed on the ancient sun dial.

He knew?

"You were married before, when you were still in your teens. He was English, and six years older than you. I believe you met in Paris. Wasn't he a painter, too?"

She turned her head slowly, wide-eyed, torn between horror and fascination at the details of her past. How much more did he know? What else had he been told?

"I won't discuss him, or the marriage, with you,"

she answered huskily. Marrying Jeremy had been a tragic mistake.

"Your father said he was after your fortune."

"And you're not?"

Lights glinted in his dark eyes. It struck her that this man would not be easily managed.

He circled her and she had to tilt her head back to see his expression. Butterflies flitted in her stomach, heightening her anxiety. He was tall, much taller than most men she'd known, and solid, a broad deep chest and muscular arms that filled the sleeves of his suit jacket.

Her nerves were on edge. She felt distinctly at a disadvantage and searched for something, anything, to give her the upperhand—again. "Good Greek men don't want to be the second husbands."

"We've already established I'm not your traditional Greek man. I do what I want, and I do it my way."

CHAPTER TWO

IT STRUCK her then, quite hard, that two could play this game. All she had to do was think like a man.

Christos Pateras wanted her to further his ambitions. He was marrying her to accomplish a goal. This wasn't about love, or emotions. This was a transaction and nothing more.

Why couldn't she approach the marriage the same way? He wanted her dowry; she wanted independence. He wanted an alliance with the Lemos family; she wanted to escape her father.

Greece might be part of a man's world but that didn't mean she had to play by a man's rules.

She sized him up again, assessing the odds. Tall, strong, ridiculously imposing, he exuded authority. Could she marry him and then slip away?

No more Alysia Lemos, poor little rich girl, but an ordinary woman with ordinary dreams. Like a small house in the country. A vegetable garden. An orchard of apple trees.

She stole a second glance at Christos's rugged profile, noting the long, straight nose, line of cheek, strong clean-shaven jaw. He looked less ruthless than determined. Assertive, not aggressive. If she ran away from him, what would he do?

Chase her down? She doubted it. He'd have too

much pride. He'd probably wait a bit and then quietly annul the marriage. Men like Christos Pateras wouldn't want to advertise their failure.

He turned, caught her eye, his dark gaze holding hers. "Everyone thinks you've already married me."

"How can that be?" she scoffed.

Opening his coat, he drew a folded newspaper from the breast pocket and handed it to her.

Not certain what she was supposed to find, she unfolded the paper and pressed the creased pages flat. Then the headlines jumped out at her, practically screaming the news. Secret Wedding For Lemos Heir.

Anger, indignation, shock flashed through her one after the other as the headlines blinded her. How could he do it? How could he pull a stunt like this?

And then just as quickly as her anger flared, inspiration struck. For the first time in months she saw an open door. All she had to do was walk through it.

Marry him, and walk away.

It was all in place. The husband, the marriage, the motivation. She just needed to go along with the plans and then leave.

Perfect. Her heart did a strange tattoo.

Maybe too perfect. Christos Pateras didn't seize control of the Greek shipping industry by luck. He was smart. No, rumor had it that he was brilliant. A brilliant man wouldn't marry a young woman and then just let her slip away. He'd be prepared. He'd be alert.

She'd have to be very, very careful.

Alarm and eagerness tangled her emotions. She could do this, she could escape him, it was a matter of being just as smart as him.

Her heart began to pound faster and she felt heat creep beneath her skin. Excitement grew but she dampened her enthusiasm, not wanting to overplay her hand or reveal her true intentions.

She frowned, feigning surprise and shock. "You can't be serious."

"It's front page news."

"There's no wedding. How can there be a story?"

"Read it for yourself."

She obliged, skimming the front page story where her father had been quoted as saying he couldn't confirm or deny reports of the secret wedding, only that he knew that Greek-American shipping tycoon, Christos Pateras, had visited Oinoussai in the past several days and had visited his daughter at the convent. Other sources confirmed that Pateras had been seen in town, while another source mentioned the convent as the secret wedding location.

Her father's work, no doubt. The puppet and the puppeteer. Incredible. But this time, she was the puppeteer. She was in control.

She crumpled the paper for show. "You and my father make a spectacular team."

"Your father's idea, not mine."

"No one will believe this drivel."

"Everyone believes it. Media has descended on the harbor. They're expecting to see the blushing bride and groom board the yacht later this afternoon.''

He looked so damn smug, as if he'd thrown a net around her, trapping her in his scheme. *Sorry, she silently apologized, but I win this one. Hands down.*

She was going to marry him. And then she'd leave him. He could pick up the pieces. The fall-out with her father wouldn't be her problem. If Christos Pateras wanted to make deals with her father, then fine, let him experience her father's wrath firsthand.

Guilt briefly assailed her. Then she ignored the voice of conscience, reminding herself that Christos and her father were the same kind of man. Selfish. Unthinking. Lacking compassion.

Not once during her mother's horrible last year did her father slow his schedule, put off a meeting, change his travel plans. He never once attended her radiation treatments. Never held her hand during the chemo. Never checked on her at night when she lay huddled with pain and fear.

Her father acted as if nothing bad had happened, ignoring the terminal diagnosis as though it were a spate of bad weather and simply charged ahead with his plans for new ships, new routes, new alliances.

Damn her father, and damn Christos Pateras.

Alysia knew of no fate worse than that of being a Greek tycoon's wife.

But she hid all this, focusing instead on her goal. Independence. Peace. A life far from the wealthy Greek shipping families. Maybe back to Geneva. Maybe a little house south of London.

"When would we marry?" she asked, her pulse leaping in anticipation.

"Today. We'd marry here, in the chapel, and then sail this afternoon."

"And just what are your expectations?"

His dark gaze studied her, his expression blank, giving away nothing. "As my wife, you'll travel with me. When I entertain, you shall perform the duties of the hostess. And for my family functions, we'll appear together, behaving like a real couple."

"Versus a business liaison?"

"Precisely."

"For your parents sake?"

"Right, again."

He didn't want to disappoint his parents. She could almost admire him for that. Almost.

But fortunately, she needn't worry about his family, or his expectations. She wouldn't be around long enough to fulfill any such duties. If they married today, this afternoon, she was just hours from freedom, hours from starting a new life for herself far from Greece and the influential Lemos name.

"Anything else?" she demanded coldly, conscious that she could never let Christos Pateras know her intentions. Christos might dress fashionably, move with athletic ease and speak eloquently, but underneath the gorgeous veneer he was the same man as her father. And her father, ruthless, critical, unyielding crushed those close to him, destroying family as indiscriminately as he destroyed friends. No one was safe. No one was exempt.

"I expect us to have a normal relationship." He, too, had become detached, businesslike.

It struck her they'd moved to the negotiation stage. The deal would take place. It was just a matter of formalizing the details. He knew it. She knew it. A bitter taste filled her mouth, but she wouldn't back down now. "Define normal, if you would."

"I expect you to be faithful. Loyal. Honest."

She felt something shift inside of her, another whisper of conscience, but she dismissed it with a small sneer. Men had controlled her all her life. For once she'd take care of herself. "That's it?"

"Should there be more?"

He was testing her, too. He knew there should be more, would be more. They hadn't even discussed the physical aspect of the marriage and it loomed there between them, heavy, forbidding.

"This is a marriage of convenience, yes?" She cast a glance at him before looking too quickly away, but she caught the predatory gleam in his eyes. He wasn't nervous. He seemed to enjoy this.

"Marriages of convenience don't produce children. I need children."

Before she could speak, he continued.

"I'll do my best, Miss Lemos, to ensure you're satisfied. I want you to be happy. It's important we're both fulfilled. Sex is a natural part of life. It should be natural between us."

Fingers of fear stroked her spine, stirring the fine hairs on her nape, even as blood surged to her face, heating her cheeks, creating a frisson of warmth through her limbs. "We hardly know each other, Mr. Pateras."

"Which is why I won't force myself on you. I'm content to wait until some of the newness wears off and we've grown more...comfortable with each other before becoming intimate."

Another surge of heat rushed to her cheeks. His voice had deepened, turning so husky as to hum within her, warm and intimate. For a split second she imagined his body against hers, his mouth against her skin.

The very thought of making love with him made her inhale sharply. Every nerve in her body seemed to be alert, aware of this man and his potent masculinity.

Crossing her arms over her chest, Alysia tried to deny the tingle in her breasts, and the longing to be real again. It'd been forever since she'd felt like a woman.

She wouldn't look at him. "You're willing to commit to a loveless marriage?"

"I'm committing to you."

Oh, to have someone want her, to care for her...

She drew a ragged breath, hope and pain twisting in her heart, seduced by his promise and the warmth in his voice. What would it feel like to be loved by this man?

She drew herself up short. He'd never said anything about love, or wanting her. He wasn't even committing to her. He was committing to the Lemos house, committing to her father, but not to her. How could she allow herself to daydream? Hadn't she learned her lesson by now?

This is how Jeremy had broken through her reserve. This is how she'd offered up her heart. Well, she couldn't, wouldn't, do it again. Experience had to count for something.

Hardening her emotions, she reminded herself that Christos Pateras did not matter. His promises did not matter. The only thing that mattered was escaping the convent and her father's manipulations. It was what her mother would want for her. It was what her mother had wanted for herself.

Glancing up, her gaze settled on the high, whitewashed wall. All convent windows faced inward, overlooking the herb garden and potted citrus trees. None of the windows faced out, no glimpse of the ocean, no picture of the world left behind...

But she hadn't left it behind. Her father had ripped it from her just weeks after her mother's death. There had been no mourning for him. Just business, just money and deals and ships.

A lump filled her throat. For a moment her chest felt raw, tight. "If we are going to do it," she said after a long painful silence, "let's not waste time."

They were married in the briefest of ceremonies in the convent chapel. Rings, exchange of vows, a passionless kiss.

In the back of the limousine, Alysia clenched her hand on her lap, doing her best to ignore the heavy diamond-and-emerald ring weighting her finger.

Christos had already told her it wasn't a family heirloom, three carat diamonds had never been part of his family fortune. No, the ring had been purchased recently, just for her. But she wouldn't wear it long. By this time tomorrow she'd have it off her finger, left behind on a dresser or bathroom counter, she promised herself.

A strange calm filled her. For the first time in years she felt as if she were in control again, acting instead of reacting, making decisions for herself instead of feeling helpless.

With a swift glance at her new husband, she noted Christos Pateras's profile, his strong brow creased, a furrow between his dark eyes. He wore his black hair combed straight back, and yet the cowlick at the temple softened the severity of his hard, proud features.

He'd be surprised—no, furious—when he discovered her gone. He didn't expect her to deceive him. It wouldn't have crossed his mind. Just like a Greek man to assume everything would go according to his plan.

He sat close to her, too close, and she inched across the seat only to have his hard thigh settle against hers again.

She became fixated on the heat passing from his thigh to hers, panic stirring at the unwelcome intimacy. She wasn't ready to be touched by him. Wasn't ready to be touched by anyone.

She scooted closer to the door, pressing herself into the corner, willing herself to shrink in size.

"You're acting like a virgin," he drawled, casting a sardonic look in her direction.

She felt like a virgin. Years and years without being touched, not even a kiss, and now this, to sit thigh to thigh with a stranger, a tall, muscular, imposing stranger who wanted her to bear his children.

Stomach heaving, Alysia pressed trembling fingers against her lips. What had she done? How could she have married him? If she didn't escape him, surely she'd die. Despite her mother's wisdom, despite the gentle counsel of the sisters, Alysia didn't want family. No children, no babies. Ever.

She couldn't ever give Christos Pateras a chance. She wouldn't let him make a move. No opportunities for seduction. First chance she could, she'd leave.

"Relax," Christos uttered flatly. "I'm not going to attack you."

She opened her eyes, glanced at him beneath lowered lashes. He looked grim, distant. Gone was the laughter, the fine creases fanning from his eyes.

The luxury sedan bounced down the narrow mountain road, the street unpaved, lurching across a deep pothole. Despite the seat belt, Alysia practically spilled into Christos's lap. Quickly she righted herself, drawing sharply away. Christos's mouth pressed tighter.

The silence stretched, tension thick. Squirming inwardly, aware that she'd helped create the hostility, Alysia searched for something to say. "You like Oinoussai?"

"It's small."

"Like America."

The corner of his mouth lifted in faint amusement. "Yes, like America." The amusement faded from his eyes, his features hardening again.

She felt his dark gaze settle on her face, studying her as dispassionately as one studied a work of art hanging on a museum wall. "Have you ever been to the States before?" he asked.

"No." She'd always wanted to go, was curious about New York and San Francisco, but she hadn't had time, nor the opportunity. Thanks to her father, she'd been too busy enjoying the special pleasures of the sanatorium and the convent.

"I have a meeting in Cephalonia, which we'll sail to from here. And then I thought we could conclude our honeymoon someplace else, someplace you might find interesting before returning to my home on the East Coast."

Honeymoon. She tensed at the very suggestion. He'd said he wouldn't force himself on her, said he'd be content to wait. Honeymooning conjured up lovemaking and intimacy and…

She shuddered. This was a mistake. She'd made a mistake. He had to turn the car around, take her back to the convent now.

"We're not going back to the convent," he said, still watching her, dark eyes hooded.

Her head snapped up. She stared at him, shocked that he knew what she'd been thinking.

"My dear Mrs. Pateras, you're not difficult to

read. You wear your emotions on your face, they're all there, right for me to see.''

He tapped her hands, knotted in her lap. ''Try to relax a little, Alysia. I'm not demanding sexual favors tonight. I'm not demanding anything from you just yet. You need time. I need time. Let's try to make this work, learn a little about each other first.''

Angered by his rational tone, finding nothing rational in being coerced into marriage, she lifted her head, temper blazing. ''You want to learn about me? Fine. I'll tell you about me. I hate Greece and I hate Greek men. I hate being treated like a second-class citizen simply because I'm a woman. I hate how money empowers the rich, creating another caste system. I hate business and the ships you treasure. I hate the alliance my father has formed with you because my father detests America and American money—'' she drew a breath, shaking from head to toe.

One of his black eyebrows lifted quizzically. ''Finished?'' he drawled.

''No. I'm not finished. I haven't even started.'' But her outburst had leveled her, and she leaned heavily against the leather upholstery, exhausted, and suddenly silent.

She wasn't used to this, wasn't used to fighting, to speaking her mind. Her father had never allowed her to say anything at all. Her father never even looked at her.

''What else is bothering you?'' Christos persisted, his attention centered on her and nothing but her.

She shook her head, unable to speak another word.

"Perhaps we should leave our philosophic differences for a later date. Those big issues can be overwhelming, hmm?" He smiled wryly, his expression suddenly human. "Why don't we start with the small things, the daily routines that give us comfort. For example, breakfast. Coffee. How do you take yours? Milk and sugar?"

She shook her head, eyes dry, gritty, throat thick. "Black," she whispered.

"No sugar?"

She shook her head again. "And yours? Black?"

"I like a touch of milk in mine." He spoke without rancor, the tone friendly, disarmingly friendly. "Are you an early riser?"

"A night owl."

"Me, too."

"Lovely," she answered bitingly. "We should be perfect together."

His expression remained blank, yet a hint of warmth lurked in his dark eyes. "A promising beginning, yes, but I do think a week or two alone should help rub some of the edges off, take the newness away. And with that in mind, I've cleared my calendar and after this meeting on Cephalonia, will have the next couple weeks free."

"How accommodating."

"I try."

Her exhaustion fed her fear. She felt a fresh wave of panic hit. What if she couldn't break away? What if he stayed too close, paid too much attention, to allow her to leave? She'd be trapped in this relationship, forced into marriage. The possibility made her almost ill, and a lump lodged in her throat, sealing it closed.

She couldn't afford to wait. She had to escape, and soon. Before boarding the yacht. Before appearing in public together.

He must have sensed her panic because he suddenly lifted her hand, examined the ring on her finger, before kissing the inside of her wrist. "You don't have to hate me."

A tremor coursed through her at the touch of his lips, her blood leaping in her veins. She tried to disengage but his mouth caressed her wrist in another sensitive spot.

"Please don't," she said, pulling at her wrist, attempting to free herself from his clasp.

"You smell like lavender and sunshine."

Anger hardened her voice. "Mr. Pateras, let me go."

He released her arm and she buried her hand in her lap. Her inner wrist burned, the skin scorched, her pulse pounding.

She hadn't realized she'd become so sensitive.

Alysia forcibly turned her attention back to the rocky landscape, watching the rough road as they snaked down the hill, kicking up dust and loose gravel. They were nearing the outskirts of town.

An unwanted thought suddenly crossed her mind. "Will I see my father in town?"

"No. He flew out this morning for a meeting in Athens."

Relief washed over her. At least she wouldn't have to deal with him right now.

"You don't care for him much, do you?" Christos asked, checking his watch and then glancing out the window again.

"No."

"He seems like a decent man."

"If you like maniacally controlling men."

His eyebrows lowered, his brow creasing. "He's tried to do what's best for you."

A lead weight dropped in her stomach. Christos Pateras didn't know the half of it! Her father had never done what's best for her. It'd always been about him.

She could forgive her father many things, but she'd never forgive him for neglecting her mother in the final weeks of her life. As her mother lay dying in that marble mausoleum of a house, Darius never once reached out to her; no acknowledgment of her pain, no interest in bringing closure, no awareness of her needs.

He should have been there for her. He owed that much to her. How could he not have cared?

A lump formed in her throat, and narrowing her eyes, Alysia concentrated very hard on the rocky landscape beyond her closed window.

"I wish I'd had the pleasure of knowing your mother."

The lead weight seemed to swell in size, pressing against her chest, making it hard to breathe. Gritty tears burned at the back of her eyes. "She was beautiful."

"I've seen photographs. She once modeled, didn't she?"

"It was a charity event. My mother was dedicated to her causes. I think if my father had let her, she would have done more." Her voice sounded thick with emotion.

"You must miss her."

Dreadfully, she thought, struggling to maintain her control. She was finding it almost impossible to juggle so many contradictory emotions at one time. The whole last year had been like this, too. The loss of her mother on top of the others...

It was too much. She sometimes didn't know where to go for strength and had to fight very hard to reach inside herself for the courage to continue.

"Your mother liked Greece?" Christos persisted.

"She tolerated it," Alysia answered huskily, patting her shift pocket for a tissue. Her eyes were watering, her nose burned, she felt like an absolute mess. And to top it all off Christos was looking at her with such concern that she felt as though she were covered in cracks, threatening to break in two.

"Too oppressive?" he mused.

"Too hot." She smiled for the first time all afternoon. Mother had hated the heat; she positively wilted in it. "Mum pined for the English grays and cool greens the way some pined for lost love."

Christos laughed softly, his expression surprisingly gentle. But his gentleness would be her undoing.

Alysia stiffened her spine, reminding herself that she couldn't trust his smile, or his warmth. He wasn't just any man; he was a man handpicked by her father and tainted.

Christos Pateras married her for money.

He was as bad, if not worse, than her father.

Flatly, no emotion left, she asked about her things. "Will I have any of my books or photos sent to me? And my wardrobe? What's happened to that?"

"Everything's already been transferred to the yacht. Your entire bedroom was boxed up and put in the ship's storage."

Shock rivaled indignation. "You're quite sure of yourself, aren't you?"

"I had your father's support."

"Obviously. But what I want to know is *how?* And why?" Her father had never liked Americans, and detested foreign money. "Why did he go to you? What made you so special?"

"I had what he needed. Money. Lots of it."

"And what did he give you in exchange?"

Christos's dark eyes gleamed at her, a faint smile playing his lips. "You."

"Aren't you lucky."

He shrugged. "Depends on how you look at it. Anyway, your father is happy. He won't bother you anymore." He turned a smoldering gaze on her. "I won't let him."

She heard the promise in his voice, and a hint of menace, too. For a moment Christos Pateras sounded like a street-boxer, an inner city thug, but then he smiled, a casual, relaxed smile, and she felt herself melt, her chilly insides warming, her fear dissipating ever so slightly. Truthfully she'd welcome a buffer between her and her father. He'd made her life nearly unbearable. She needed to get away.

Elegant whitewashed villas came into view, along with the sparkling harbor waters. The late-afternoon sun illuminated the bay. "There's my yacht," Christos said, leaning forward to point out a breathtaking ship of luxurious proportions.

She leaned forward, too, her breath catching in her throat. The yacht might prove to be just as confining as the convent and it crossed her mind that she might have bitten off more than she could chew.

No, she'd be fine. She'd figured a way out. She simply needed time.

Numerous fishing boats dotted the harbor, as did several yachts, but one moored ship dwarfed all others. The glossy white, sleek design only hinted at the elegant state rooms inside. The yacht would have cost him dearly.

She didn't realize she'd spoken the thought out loud until he chuckled softly, a twisted smile at his lips. "She was expensive, but not half as much as you."

Indignation heated her skin, hot color sweeping through her cheeks. "You didn't buy me, Mr. Pateras, you bought my father!"

But he was right about one thing, Alysia thought darkly as the limousine pulled up to the harbor. The media were out, and out in force. Reporters and photographers crawled all over town, jostling each other to take better position.

They surged forward when the car stopped and she sucked in a panicked breath. All those cameras poised...all the microphones turned on...

"It'll be over in a minute," Christos said, turning to her.

She felt his inspection, his dark eyes examining her face, her dress, her hair. He startled her by reaching up to pluck pins from her hair. The heavy honey mass tumbled down and he combed his fingers through it with unnerving familiarity.

"That's better," he murmured.

Just the touch of his fingers against her brow sent shivers racing through her. Repulsion, she told herself, even as the tight core of her warmed, softened. She didn't want him. Couldn't want him.

But when he tucked one long silky strand behind her ear, his hand caressing the ear, then the tender spot below, her belly ached and her limbs felt terrifyingly weak.

No one had touched her so gently in years.

Her need shocked her. She felt like a woman starved for food and warmth. Helplessly she gazed at him, hating herself for responding to him. "Are you quite finished?" she whispered breathlessly.

"No, not quite," he murmured, before his dark head lowered.

She stiffened as his head dropped, drawing back against the leather upholstery. *No!* No, no, no. He couldn't do this, couldn't kiss her, especially not here, not when she felt like this. Everything was too new, too strange, too crazy.

If he felt her resistance, he ignored it, clasping the back of her head, fingers twining in her long hair. She caught the glint in his dark eyes and a hint of rich, sweet spice. Not vanilla, not cinnamon, but some other fragrance so deep, and familiar, that it tantalized her memory.

His mouth took possession of hers and she breathed him in again, reminded of almonds, sweet baby powder, the heady musk of antique roses...

Somehow it all fit, he, this, the kiss. His mouth, the warmth of his skin, the strength in his arms. Tremor after tremor coursed through her veins, creating an intense craving for more sensation.

Even as his lips parted hers, another electric current shot through her, sparking awareness in every nerve in her body. More, her brain demanded, her lips moving beneath his, her tongue answering the play of his, more, more...

The kiss deepened, and unconsciously she moved against him seeking to prolong the contact, relishing the hard plane of his chest, the warmth of his skin, the heady sweet spice of his cologne.

As his tongue sought the sensitive hollows in her mouth, the inside of her lip, the curve of cheek, blood pooled in her lower belly, her veins pulsing. This felt, he felt...

Incredible.

Muffled voices penetrated her brain. Voices. People.

Her eyes flew open, reality returning.

Cameras pressed against the limousine windows, dozens of lenses, shutters snapping. "Mr. Pateras, we have company."

He raised his head, his mouth curving into a satisfied smile. He didn't even give the throng of reporters a second glance. "Let them watch. After all, this is what they've come for."

Panicked, she tried to bolt from the car, lunging out thinking only of running from the crowd and the cameras and Christos—

A hand clamped at her waist, biting into her skin, holding her still. "Mrs. Pateras—" Christos's husky voice pierced her panic "—smile for the cameras."

CHAPTER THREE

LEAVING the noisy media throng behind, Alysia stepped aboard the yacht, late-afternoon sun glinting off the water in the purest form of golden light.

Christos swiftly introduced her to his staff and crew, rattling off the dozen names, even as the yacht gently swayed in the harbor waters.

The emotionally intense afternoon, the numerous introductions, the strangeness of her new surroundings suddenly exhausted her. Or was it the stark realization that until they touched land, she was really and truly caught in this pretend marriage?

She might never get away.

She might be trapped forever.

Her head swimming, she gulped air, panic overriding every other thought. What had she done? What in God's name had she done?

"I can't," she choked, searching for the exit, her gaze jumping from wall to door to patch of blue sky outside. "I can't do this, I can't, I can't—"

"You can," Christos softly countered, stepping closer to her side. "You already did."

He cut the introductions short and took her by the elbow, steering her through the formal salon to an elegant stateroom decorated in the palest shades of blue. Just beyond the wide French doors, the ocean shimmered a brilliant royal-blue. The effect was calming, indescribably peaceful, and she relaxed slightly.

"Do you need a drink?" he asked, sliding his suit jacket off.

"No."

"Brandy might help."

Nothing would help, she thought, not until she got off the yacht. But she couldn't say that, and she couldn't allow him to become suspicious.

Christos tossed his jacket across the foot of the bed. "Maybe a long hot bath would feel good. I can't imagine you were allowed such indulgences in the convent."

"No, definitely not. Cold showers were de rigueur."

He began unfastening the top button on his fine dress shirt. "Think you'll be comfortable here?"

Her gaze took in the massive bed with the bolsters and mountain of pillows. Soft silk drapes hung at the French doors. The same ice-blue silk covered a chaise lounge. Her fingertips caressed the silk chaise, the down-filled cushion giving beneath the weight of her hand. Her room at the convent had been so spartan. "Yes."

"Good." He continued unfastening one small button after another, revealing first his throat and then his darkly tanned chest with the crisp curl of hair.

Alysia sucked in a breath, the glimpse of his chest hair so personal she felt as if she'd invaded his privacy. Yet she found herself turning to watch him again, half-fascinated, half-fearful. Christos appeared utterly at ease as he slipped the shirt from his shoulders, the smooth muscular planes of his chest rippling.

"Your wardrobe's in the closet," he added. "Do change into something more comfortable. We'll have a light meal now on the deck and then supper later, closer to ten."

The typical Greek dinner hour. But not the typical Greek man. She quickly averted her gaze again.

Then his words registered. *Your wardrobe's in the closet.* "We share this room?"

His expression didn't change. "Of course."

She took a defensive step backward, bumping the edge of the writing table. She glanced down at the desk's polished surface, noting the neat arrangement of paper, inkwell, pen. "Mr. Pateras, you know the terms of our agreement."

"Sharing a bed isn't a sexual act, Mrs. Pateras."

"It's close enough."

"Surely you've shared a room before."

He didn't mention her former husband. He didn't need to. She knew exactly what he was thinking and she didn't like his presumption. "Regardless, I'd like a room of my own, please."

He walked toward her. She leaned back, her bottom bumping the desk. Without apology, he took her in his arms, his mouth covering hers.

Heat flooded her veins, heat swept through her middle, into her belly and deeper still. She felt hot and weak and when he parted her lips with his, she didn't resist. If anything she opened her mouth wider, arched closer, straining against the emptiness since her mother's death, and the years before.

His palm found her hip, pressed her more tightly against him. She felt the thrust of his arousal and her breasts ached, nipples hardening. This was too close but not close enough, too much sensation and yet too little, everything felt hot and flushed and yet it was wrong.

But she didn't pull away, couldn't pull away, riveted by the tumult of her feelings.

His tongue flicked against her inner lower lip before exploring the recesses of her mouth. Teeth grazed teeth, and then he bit once into the softness of her lip. Her protest sounded like a whimper, more desire than denial, and Christos made a sound low in his throat, rough, hungry.

He was tasting her, exploring, setting her body and limbs on fire. No pretend marriage for him. He'd have her naked and beneath him in no time.

Her legs were trembling and she felt the fire lick her ankles, her knees, between her thighs. It was, she thought wildly, a fire she didn't want, wouldn't be able to control.

Christos broke the kiss off, lifting his dark head to gaze into her eyes. He trailed a finger down her flushed cheek. "Separate rooms?" he said hoarsely. "I don't think so."

Christos left to speak with the captain and Alysia fled to the shower. Inside the glass stall, water streamed from the showerhead and she soaped her face vigorously, determined to wash away every trace of Christos's kisses.

Who did he think he was, kissing her, touching her, treating her like one of his possessions?

He might have made a deal with her father, but he hadn't made a deal with her! With another swipe of the soapy washcloth, she scrubbed her mouth again and then her neck, shoulders, breasts.

It had been ages since she'd indulged in a long, hot shower and she lathered her hair in the fragrant shampoo provided. The rich scent reminded her of a fruit cocktail with its fragrance of citrus, mango, papaya. It formed billowy suds and rinsed easily.

Christos Pateras spared no expense of anything. Yachts. Wives. Or bath necessities.

Suddenly the yacht hummed to life, the engine's vibrations shooting through the white ceramic floor tiles into the soles of her feet. They were leaving Oinoussai at last!

With one towel wrapped around her body, and another twisted turban-style around her head, she padded quickly to the bedroom.

Ambivalent emotions whirled within her, her breath catching in a mix of excitement and dread. She'd waited so long to leave Oinoussai, but to leave as an American's wife!

As the yacht pulled anchor she felt momentum shift in her own life. Anything could happen now.

Everything could happen now.

In mute satisfaction, she watched Oinoussai recede, the small island shrinking small, smaller, small-

est until miles of water lay between the yacht and
the rocky sweep of land.

Finally the island became just a speck in the sea,
and then disappeared altogether. When the island was
gone, and the horizon blue, just endless blue water
and a low, gold sun starting to set, Alysia released
the bottled air in her lungs in a rush, her eyes sting-
ing, her heart thumping, lungs raw and bursting.

She inhaled another breath and suddenly it all became easier, freer, as if a weight had toppled from
her chest.

Free. She was free. She might have been back on
Oinoussai only two years, but those years felt like
forever. It had been forever. Not just her mother's
death, but the sanatorium, the horrible marriage to
Jeremy, the baby…

The baby.

Alysia sank onto the bed, crushing the ice-blue silk
coverlet. Groaning, she covered her face with her
hands, pressing the heel of her palms to her eyes.
Miniature yellow dots exploded against the blackness
of her lids.

Her heart felt as if it were on fire and the pain
consumed her. With a strangled sob, she rocked back
and forth, stricken with need, tortured by the memory.

Alexi, I miss you, I miss you, I miss you.

It was too much, too sharp, too horrible.

She couldn't do this, couldn't give in to the terrible
grief again. The doctors at the sanatorium had taught
her to fight back, to keep the memories at bay.

Grinding her palms against her eyes, she pressed until she could see nothing, hear nothing, remember nothing.

Little by little she calmed, still rocking herself on the bed, unconsciously mimicking the motion she'd used to soothe Alexi when he couldn't get comfortable, when sleep seemed impossible. Back and forth, back and forth, until at last the monster inside her slept.

And slowly the grief receded until it lay still and silent, a great hulking giant at memory's gate.

Drawing a painful breath, she slowly lifted her head, catching a glimpse of herself in the large gold-framed mirror hanging above the antique chest of drawers.

Wide, wild eyes. Trembling lips. Terror there, hatred, too.

How could she not be full of hate? She'd done a terrible, unforgivable thing. She hated no one more than she hated herself.

Christos watched her appear on the deck, a vision in the palest shade of pink. Her long thin sleeveless dress clung to her breasts, brushed her ankles, sliding over her slim hips. With her long wheat and honey hair pulled into a knot at her nape, she looked incredibly feminine, very fragile, and he felt a wave of possession sweep through him. She was his now. She belonged to him.

He'd seen her before, years ago, at a gathering in Athens. She was young, even more blond, and she'd entered the room to tearfully whisper something to her father.

The men had hushed, the meeting interrupted, and Darius Lemos reacted in anger. He slapped his daughter in front of everyone, the sound of his palm loud, too loud in the suddenly silent room.

Christos had been twenty-seven and the foreigner, the interloper, alienated at the back of the room. Although he spoke fluent Greek, he hadn't understood all the innuendoes tossed his way. All he knew was that he'd had his fill of poverty, and powerlessness, and he'd never let anyone dictate to him again.

He'd been shocked when Darius struck his daughter, the savagery of the blow leaving a vivid handprint on the girl's face. But the girl hadn't made a sound. She simply stared at her father, tears swimming in her eyes, before wordlessly leaving the room.

The meeting resumed and all continued as if nothing happened.

But something happened. Something happened to Christos.

Alysia approached him now as slowly, as hesitantly as she'd approached her father all those years ago.

Silently he handed her a glass of champagne, noting as he did the spiky tips of her sooty lashes, the dampness at the corners of her startling blue-green eyes. She'd been crying.

"Second thoughts?" he murmured.

"And thirds, and fourths." She turned her head away, revealing more of her creamy nape.

Again he felt the urge to take her in his arms, to kiss her soft skin and make her warm in his hands. He'd know her better than anyone one day. He'd discover all the secrets she kept buried within her.

She rested her slender arms on the railing, the glass of champagne ignored, dangling in her fingers. The yacht was moving swiftly through the water and the wind lifted tendrils of hair from her smooth knot.

"Where are we going?" she asked.

"Where do you want to go?"

"Away from Greece."

"Done."

She turned her head just enough to glance at him over her bare pale shoulder. Her skin gleamed. Her blue eyes were dark, mysterious. "I don't even know where you live."

"We'll live outside New York most of the time. But I also have houses in London, Provence and on the Amalfi Coast."

"You sound restless."

Amusement curved his mouth. "See, you know me already."

The uniformed cabin steward stepped onto the deck, signaling that the light meal was ready. Christos held out a hand, gesturing for Alysia to follow the cabin steward to the table set on the far end of the deck.

Christos held her chair as she took her place at the

small table on the deck. "You look beautiful in pink."

She set her champagne glass down, pushing it across the linen cloth toward the floral centerpiece. She waited until the steward stepped away to speak. Very carefully she kept her gaze fixed on the yellow and white roses. "Let's not pretend this is anything but a business arrangement, Mr. Pateras."

"By its very nature, marriage is a business arrangement." He sat down across from her and leaned back in his chair. "But that doesn't mean it has to be sterile, or cold and intolerable. Nor does it mean we can't celebrate our union."

She grasped the stem of the champagne flute between two fingers. "And what are we celebrating, Mr. Pateras? Your new financial gain? Your alliance with Darius Lemos?"

"All of the above."

She made a move to set her glass down. "Then I'd rather not."

"What if we celebrate your beauty then?"

"I definitely won't drink to that."

"You don't think you're beautiful?"

"I know I'm not."

"I find you breathtaking."

"Perhaps you've lacked for company, lately."

He smiled, almost indulgently. "I've had exceptional company. But you, I must admit, fascinate me. You're a tormented beauty, aren't you?"

She paled, her eyes growing enormous, her blue

irises dark and flecked with bits of bottle-green. "This conversation makes me very uncomfortable."

"Sorry."

But he didn't sound sorry, she thought, fighting fresh panic, feeling increasingly trapped.

While dressing tonight she'd determined to keep her distance, to remain detached, to do everything in her power to keep him at arm's length but his power was insidious. She found herself drawn to him in ways she couldn't fathom.

He was a stranger. He'd been bought by her father. He only wanted Lemos money. So why did her heart stir and her emotions twist, why did she want what was absolutely wrong for her?

She half closed her eyes, reminding herself that he was a spider and he'd woven a web and if she weren't careful he'd eat her, the same way a spider ate a little fly.

This was about survival.

Alysia crossed one ankle behind the other, as if to fortify herself, become impenetrable. She'd shut him out, draw the line here. He wouldn't cross it. She wouldn't let him.

Christos stirred, lazily stretching out one long arm to drag her chair toward him. He had no intention of letting her escape. "No need to be frightened."

"I'm not." Good, frost glittered in her voice.

"Your pulse is racing. I can see it there, at your throat."

Her heart was racing. She felt breathless, dizzy, on edge. If he touched her, she'd scream. If he drew her any closer, she'd leap out of her skin. This was all going wrong, terribly wrong and there was nothing she could do now but play the cards she'd been given.

"It's not. I'm quite calm. You probably need glasses."

His lips tightened and then eased and she realized he was grinning. "My vision is perfect. Twenty/twenty. Neither my father nor mother wear glasses, either." His smile faded, eyebrows pulling and suddenly all laughter was gone and he looked hard, focused, determined. "Why do you think so little of yourself?"

The swift change of subject knocked her off balance. Alysia felt as though she'd run smack into a wall and she shook her head once, dazed by the contact with a reality she resisted.

Why, he asked? Because she'd committed an act so terrible, so vile that her husband had left her, her friends abandoned her, her mind had shut down. It had taken her time in the sanatorium to begin to recover.

"You're intelligent, beautiful, sensitive, possibly charming," he said, touching her on the cheek with the back of his hand. She averted her head. He took her chin in his hand and turned her back to face him. "Why so little pride?"

The kindness in his voice almost undid her. No one except her mother, and maybe the abbess, had spoken to her so softly, so gently, in years. He made her feel like a...human being.

Tears started in her eyes and she blinked them back. Clutching the champagne flute's slender stem even more tightly, she tried to break the intensity of his gaze. "Please, no more."

"I want to understand."

"There's nothing to understand. I am what my father says I am. Reckless. Disobedient. Rebellious."

His dark gaze moved searchingly across her face, examining every inch of her profile before dropping to her breasts and lower still. "Are you?"

"Of course. I'm my father's daughter."

She'd meant to be flippant but it came out dreadfully wrong, more despair than arrogance in her husky voice. Suddenly she felt completely naked, her dress no more protection than a sheet of plastic kitchen wrap.

Alysia clutched the champagne flute as though her life depended on it. What if he discovered the truth about her? What if he realized the kind of person she really was? "Let me go, please. You can keep the dowry, my jewels, my savings. I don't want anything."

"You couldn't survive poor. You've never tasted poverty. It tastes as bad as it looks."

"I'd rather be poor and free. *Please*, just let me go."

His dark gaze bored through her. He didn't speak for a long, tense moment. Finally he shook his head. "I can't. I need you too much."

Her slim body jerked, her hand convulsively tightened on the goblet and with an ear-splitting pop, she snapped the crystal stem in two. The champagne flute crashed in pieces to the table. A shard of glass lodged painfully deep in her thumb.

It was like slow motion, she thought, watching the blood suddenly spurt in a brilliant red stream. Christos swore violently, sounding every bit a native Greek, as he grabbed a linen napkin and covered the arc of blood.

"I'm fine," she protested weakly.

"You're not. You're a bleeding fountain." He lifted the napkin briefly to inspect the damage. "You might need stitches."

"It'll stop."

He cast her a scathing glance. "There's glass in it. Hold still."

Eyebrows flat, expression grim, his lips compressed, he probed the wound, gently working the sliver from her tender thumb. She winced at the pressure and he caught her grimace. Suddenly his expression changed. His eyes were so dark, so deep they looked bottomless. "I don't want to hurt you."

"You didn't hurt me. I did it myself."

"Still."

Still. As though he had the power to somehow heal all wounds, restore her peace of mind and soothe the cuts and bruises. Not just a groom, but a miracle man. Wouldn't that be something? Tears sprang to her eyes and she bit into her lower lip overwhelmed by the intensity of her longing to feel whole and rested, more herself again.

Christos tossed the glass shard onto the tablecloth.

"That should do it," he said, wiping away the drying blood and bandaging her thumb.

She held her breath as he tucked the ends of the linen cloth beneath the edge of the bandage. Something about his touch made her feel too warm, too liquid. He made her feel so...safe. What an illusion. Could anything be more unjust?

"Your father told me you're not to be trusted," Christos glanced up into her face, black lashes only partly lifting, his expression concealed. "But I didn't know he meant with my crystal."

His lips quirked, a black eyebrow arched, but beneath his ironic tone, she heard concern, then immediately chided herself. This is a deal, a marriage deal and you are a very expensive bride.

Her throat sealed shut. Unable to speak she stared at his hands, the backs very broad and tanned, his fingers long and well-tapered. His touch was so light, so deft, he could have been a carpenter, or a surgeon. Legally he was her husband. *Husband.* A shiver raced down her spine, and yet it wasn't fear creating havoc, it was anticipation. Her imagination was running riot. Nervously she glanced up into his face and her heart skittered sideways, as if she was a frightened country mouse instead of one of the wealthiest women in Greece. But money didn't equate with confidence, or happiness. No one knew that better than she. "My father...he told you I wasn't to be trusted?"

"Mmm."

A blush of shame rose to her cheeks. What else

had her father told him? She knew too well that her
father's honesty could be brutal. He had hurt her, and
her mother, countless times with his cutting ap-
praisal. No one was good enough for him. Certainly
not his family.

"Don't," Christos said, his voice unusually husky
as he reached up to brush her flushed cheek with the
tip of his finger.

A strange pain flickered through her and she
pressed her bandaged hand to her belly. Everything
felt so raw just then, so exposed. She could smell the
sharp pungent salt in the air, the warmth of the night,
the motion of the ship as it surged through the waves.
"Don't what?"

"Think." Grooves formed on either side of his
mouth, small creases fanned from the corners of his
eyes. "You're torturing yourself again."

"Better me than you." She smiled as carelessly as
possible, a devil-be-damned smile that hurt in every
pore of her body. She'd fought her demons before
and won. She'd win again. And she'd do it without
Christos's help, or interference, whatever it might be.

"One more quick check," he insisted, taking her
hand and lifting the edge of the napkin to examine
the cut as if it were a wound of significance. "Maybe
you won't need stitches after all."

"Thank you, Doctor."

"My pleasure."

He should have laughed, grinned, said something
lighthearted. Instead he stared into her eyes, earnest
and focused, deep furrows marring his high bronze

brow. She swore he could see right through her. See her fears, her shocking secrets.

The blood drained from her face, the intensity of his gaze unnerving. What did he see when he looked at her like that? What did he possibly know? She felt threads of panic, hints of the past. "Really, Christos, I won't fall apart over this." She'd meant to be funny, to ease the tension, but he didn't even crack a smile.

His jaw flexed, a small muscle pulling near his ear. "First time you've used my given name."

What was he doing to her? Softening her stony heart, breaking through her defenses, that's what he was doing. She couldn't allow it, wouldn't let him dismantle the high, hard wall she'd built around herself. No one came inside. Ever.

The sooner they reached Cephalonia, the better. Alysia pushed back her chair, and rose unsteadily. "I don't think I'm hungry. If you'll excuse me, I'd like to return to my room."

"Certainly. Why don't you go to our room and rest. I'll have dinner sent to you later."

CHAPTER FOUR

AFTER her solitary dinner, Alysia changed into her satin lilac pajama set, the wide trousers and loose jacket style top covering her from ankles to collarbone. Of all her pajamas these were the least figure-flattering and not at all bridelike.

Bride. Even the word stuck in her throat, making her gag. But she wasn't a bride. She was an impostor and this time tomorrow she'd be gone. Christos could have the marriage annulled and they'd both put this embarrassing episode behind them.

Alysia crawled into bed and tried to sleep, but sleep didn't come. Moonlight flickered through the gap in the curtains and the rocking of the yacht was doing funny things to her insides. She felt deceptively warm, and alive, nerve endings alert, senses sharp. Turning onto her side, she closed her eyes and listened to the slap of waves against the yacht's hull, the groan and creak of wood and the low hum of the engine. Would Christos put in an appearance? Did he intend to share the bed?

How could she think she could manage a man like Christos Pateras? She must have been out of her mind. He might not be exactly like her father, but he was close enough. He'd get what he wanted and he wanted children.

61

Her stomach cramped and she squeezed her eyes shut. Don't panic, she soothed. Tomorrow they'd dock in Cephalonia, the largest of the Ionian islands, and mountainous Cephalonia was diverse enough, busy enough, to allow her to escape and hide. She just had to wait for the right opportunity.

Calmer, Alysia relaxed, and gave herself over to the gentle roll and sway of the ship. The rocking motion soon lulled her to sleep.

Warmth permeated her dreams, as well as the realization that a very solid, very real presence was taking up more than half of the bed.

Opening her eyes she discovered Christos next to her, his long muscular body inches away, his arm outstretched, practically touching her.

Alysia stiffened, held her breath, as his palm moved slowly across her head to tangle briefly in the long strands of hair. As quietly as possible, she scooted away, creeping to the bed's edge and listening with satisfaction as his hand fell to the mattress.

Alysia gathered her hair, moving it from harm's way. His deep, steady breathing reassured her and little by little she relaxed. Just when she was close to drifting off again, Christos stirred.

Suddenly he moved against her, pressing his thighs to the back of her legs. Total body contact, hip to ankle, his knees fitting behind hers, his groin pressed to her bottom.

Despite the clamor of protest inside her head, her body came to life, nerve endings screaming as if electrified.

Opening her eyes, she gripped the downy comforter, and stared at the edge of the bed, then down at the carpet. There was nowhere to go. She bit her knuckle to keep from shouting out loud.

She wasn't ready for this kind of intimacy. She didn't know Christos, and couldn't bear to be pressed limb to limb with him.

As her senses flooded, responding to his heat and strength, her fear grew. She'd never met a man who aroused such contradictory emotions in her before. Awareness, mistrust, desire, dread.

Using her elbow, she pushed against his chest, trying to prod him backward. He didn't budge. She pushed again. And still nothing but his deep, even breathing, his warm breath bathing the back of her neck.

Damn him. Damn his incredible nerve. Damn his empire, too.

He had her trapped on the edge of the bed. She couldn't move forward, she'd fall on the floor. If she wiggled backward, and she tried, she came up square against his groin.

Suddenly she realized not all of him was asleep.

Part of him was definitely awake and his thin cotton pajama pants did nothing to contain his impressive length.

Mortified, she pressed a forearm across her eyes, trying to block out the pressure of his arousal against her bottom. But the more she denied the existence of his erection the more rigid his shaft became, enflaming her tender skin, creating heat and liquid desire between her thighs.

The tip of his erection strained against her night-wear, her thighs tingling, her innermost muscles tightening, clenching at air and nothing when he lay so dangerously close.

She'd never admit it in a thousand years, but she wanted him, wanted to feel more of him, and the carnal want was more than she could bear. She'd never been physical, never felt sexual in her life, but Christos Pateras was changing all that. He was making her ache for things she'd never fully experienced.

Alysia writhed. She couldn't help it. She only prayed he was so deeply asleep he didn't know the effect he was having on her. Wriggling, her hips shifted, and she brushed the tip of his shaft, tormenting herself.

In the dark, with her arms around herself, and his arousal square against her, she could imagine making love to him, imagine him inside of her, imagine the pleasure of being filled by him.

It was all she could do to not whimper aloud.

And still, he slept on.

Suddenly one of his arms snaked out and clasped her around the waist, holding her firmly against him. His chest pressed to her back. His hips formed a cradle for her bottom. His taut thighs shaped hers. His shaft nearly pierced her through the satin of her pajamas.

Her heart stuttered, her breath caught in her throat. Digging her teeth into her soft lower lip, she muffled a groan. This was torture. Exquisite torture of the best and worst kind.

"Go to sleep," Christos growled in the darkness, his voice pitched deep and rough.

"I can't."

"You can. Just close your eyes. Stop thinking."

Thinking! She wasn't thinking. She was feeling, and every nerve ending begged for more sensation. She felt wired for action and nothing was happening. Absolutely nothing. So how was she supposed to sleep?

It seemed as if she lay awake for hours, her lower belly aching, her inner muscles clenching at nothing.

Easy for him to say sleep, he wasn't the one about to explode out of her skin. But finally, painfully, she drifted off. When she next awoke, the sun was shining and Christos was gone.

Dressing in a slim taupe linen skirt and matching knit top, Alysia tried to deny the nervous thrill she felt at seeing Christos again. He'd made her feel desperate last night, his hard muscled body a torment, and yet he'd also been warm. And solid. And real.

She thrust her feet into strappy tan sandals and hurried upstairs to the deck. A steward met her, greeted her with a bow and showed her to the breakfast table overflowing with lavish platters of fresh fruit and sweet rolls, yogurt and coffee. But no sign of Christos.

She felt her excitement plummet, anticipation turning inside out. The disappointment was so strong that she felt furious with herself for caring so much about someone she knew so little. For heaven's sake, he was a stranger. She married him to escape her father, not for a stab at domestic tranquillity.

Alysia nearly dropped her china coffee cup. She wasn't falling for him, was she? She didn't really expect a happy-ever-after with him…did she? This wasn't a real marriage. It wasn't a honeymoon.

Wake up, she snapped at herself. *Grow up!*

Halfway through her croissant, her appetite well and truly gone, she spotted gleaming white bobbing next to the ship on the water. Pushing back from her chair she moved to the railing and looked down. A speedboat.

Sleekly designed, painted a glossy white and maroon, the speedboat hadn't been there before. Had someone come on board? Or was Christos planning a trip out?

Either way, there was a boat, and means for escape.

Her fingers tightened on the railing, the wood warmed by the sun. She felt a whisper of regret, but mocked her weakness and her attraction to a man so potentially dangerous. This wasn't the time to rely on her emotions. She needed to act.

Swiftly descending the flight of stairs that joined the two wraparound decks, Alysia slid over the bottom rail and into the low-slung speedboat. She reached past the steering wheel toward the gauges. A key dangled from the ignition. *Yes.*

A shadow darkened the deck, filtering the bright

morning sun. "Going somewhere?" a husky voice drawled.

Christos.

Her stomach fell so fast and hard she leaned against the speedboat's dash, fingers compulsively flexing.

Go, just go, a terrified voice screamed inside her head. Get out of here.

But she couldn't move, paralyzed by fear. She stiffened, expecting him to grab her, haul her from the boat. He'd be enraged. He'd be physical.

"You like the Donzi?" he asked, his voice husky, almost amused.

How could he be amused? She'd tried to run away.

"The Donzi?" she choked, her breathing ragged, her body weighted with fear, and dread. Her father would have broken her in two if she'd tried this with him.

"My speedboat. It's an American boat, made in Florida."

Tensing, she dragged her gaze up, an inch at a time. He was wearing faded khaki shorts that exposed every sinewy muscle in his thigh and calf and a white cotton T-shirt that had obviously seen better days.

He looked fearless, careless, distinctly American. A frisson of warmth shot through her. There was no anger in his eyes. No anger in the twist of his lips.

"Get your swimsuit," he said, stepping down into the boat, one long bare leg grazing hers. "I've got a favorite beach I like to visit whenever I'm near Cephalonia.''

She almost tripped in her haste to escape him. ''I'm not much for the beach,'' she fibbed, scrambling out of the boat, away from him, cursing her slim-fitting skirt that hindered her movement.

Christos watched her struggles with interest, arms folded across his chest, the white T-shirt pulled taut at the shoulders. ''This isn't an elective, Mrs. Pateras. It's a requirement. Get your suit. We're going swimming.''

Heaping Greek curses on his head, Alysia changed in the bedroom, stepping out of her panties and bra and into a two-piece bathing suit she hadn't worn in years. Except for the bare midriff, the tank-style suit was cut conservatively, a little high on the thigh, but not indecently so, the top more like a soft sports bra, ample coverage there, too.

This shouldn't do much for Mr. Pateras, she thought, glimpsing her slim pale limbs in the mirror, her arms too long, her legs too thin, her head looking ridiculously doll-like on her fragile body.

She didn't look much like a Greek woman anymore, her curves melting away. Nursing her mother had taken its toll, the long exhausting hours decimating what little remained of her appetite. No wonder the sisters were always telling her to eat. She wasn't just slender anymore, she was skinny.

Alysia resolved to eat better starting immediately. No more cups of black coffee and nibbles of croissant for breakfast. She'd eat more fruit and vegetables, take bigger portions, make sure she was getting enough of the healthy foods.

The telephone by the bed rang and Alysia started. It rang again and she reached for it.

It was Christos. "Are you coming up or do I need to fetch you?"

"I'm coming," she retorted grimly before slamming the phone back down. She was definitely going back up. The last thing she needed was to be alone with Christos in the bedroom again.

Christos untied the speedboat from the yacht and within minutes they were jumping the white-tipped waves, sending streams of water into the air. The wind whipped Alysia's long hair into a frenzy, and she grabbed at it, futilely trying to bring it under control.

The speedboat hit a big teal-green wave and Alysia threw her hands out to steady herself.

Grinning, Christos shot her a quick glance. "Too fast?" he shouted.

"No!" The speed dazzled her, nearly as much as the brilliant sunshine and intense sparkle of blue water. She felt immersed in sensation—the speed of the boat, the surge of the engine, the wind whipping through her hair. Could she feel any more alive?

"You must have spent a lot of time on the water with your father," Christos said, his voice breaking up in the wind.

"Not really. He doesn't really like sailing. He usually flies everywhere he needs to go."

They were flying over the water now. Salty spray

coating her skin, droplets dancing in her hair. The daring capabilities of the Donzi left her breathless. "This is incredible," she confessed. "I could get addicted to this."

Christos laughed, the sound deep, husky and something turned over in Alysia's chest. She could see herself cradled in his arms, snuggled against his chest as she'd been last night. He'd been so warm and strong, his hard body a refuge.

Fiercely she squashed the image, reminding herself that he'd forced her into this marriage, manipulated her into taking vows. This wasn't a real relationship. He'd *bought* her.

Her pleasure in the boat ride faded and she sat numbly for the remainder of the trip. When Christos slowed the Donzi to steer into a protected little bay, Alysia felt tears prick her eyes. He made everything seem so interesting. His voice resonated with warmth and she found herself responding to him over and over again.

It made her mad. No, furious. And not just at him, but at herself. Didn't she have any sense? What about her self-control?

The boat motored closer to shore. The bay, shaped by massive rocks and backed by rugged vegetation, looked utterly private. No roads, no other boats, no people. Just the crescent beach with powdery ivory sand and the gentle lapping of waves.

They were alone. Completely alone.

Panic shot through her. Panic because this secluded little beach was nothing short of a lover's paradise. Picnic lunch, leisurely swim and exquisite lovemaking on the pristine sand.

Christos shifted and turning she caught a glimpse of him pulling his T-shirt over his head. His lifted arms tightened his chest, his rippled abdominal muscles contracted. His flat stomach was so lean and hard she itched to trace each sinewy muscle with her finger. A peculiar sensation rippled through her.

More desire, fresh desire flooded her, her breasts lifting with her swift intake. She felt an ache at the juncture of her thighs, her body suddenly hot and weak all over. She wanted something from him no man had ever given her. Wanted something that until now she didn't even know existed.

Tossing his T-shirt down, Christos looked at her, their eyes meeting. His dark gaze locked with hers, and in his eyes she realized he knew what she was feeling, and that he was feeling it, too.

Her tummy clenched, her nipples hardened, her mouth full and sensitive. All from just one look.

If he touched her she'd melt. She'd puddle at his feet and beg for release. She'd clutch his wrist and move his hand across her body, across her stomach, to cup her breasts and then down again, over her hips to her thighs. She'd show him every spot that tingled. She'd press her mouth to his, taste his skin, drink him in—

Good God, what was happening here?

Jerkily Alysia rose, turned, covered her parted lips and shook her head. No, no, no. Not like this, not here, not with him.

She felt the boat rock and then heard a splash. Christos was in the water. He waded to the beach, tied the speedboat to an iron ring drilled in one of the massive rock formations.

He returned to the boat and reach for her. "Let me give you a hand."

"Don't touch me!" Color washed her cheeks. She sounded absolutely terrified.

His eyes narrowed, thick black lashes concealing his expression. "You okay?"

No. She wasn't okay. She was anything but okay. Her heart felt strange and her emotions were wild and she didn't know what was happening to her but she was losing control, felt sickeningly out of control, and this wasn't supposed to happen. Not with him.

It'd been over four years since her marriage to Jeremy ended and in all those years she hadn't been with another man. Four years had passed since she'd last been touched, kissed, caressed. Four years of nothing and now she felt absolutely crazy with sensation.

"I can manage," she choked, resenting the fact that he stirred her up, that he *mattered*.

Christos shrugged, his lips compressed, and without a word gathered the picnic basket and towels from inside the boat and headed back to shore.

Alysia sat in the tethered boat, hands knotted in her lap and watched him drop the basket and towels into the sand before he returned to the water to swim. As the boat bobbed she followed his progress. He was a strong swimmer, his long, toned arms slicing through the waves, his dark head turning at regular intervals for air.

He'd covered the bay, reached the far end of the cove and prepared to turn around. Alysia pulled off her skirt and top and dived over the edge of the boat, swimming quickly to shore. The water actually felt wonderful, not too warm or too cold, just refreshing.

On the beach she toweled off, and then spread her towel to dry. She sat down on her damp towel and watched Christos's approach. He was on his back now, lazily swimming along the shore. His dark head was thrown back, his muscular arms rotating in impossibly smooth arcs.

Poseidon. God of the Ocean.

Suddenly another boat motored into the bay and anchored not far from Christos's Donzi. The group piled out, several families it seemed, mothers spreading blankets and towels on the sand, while the children splashed in the surf. The fathers sat together, a circle of male authority and Alysia darkly noted that while the men sat, the women did all the work. Typical.

Christos waded out of the ocean, water streaming, dark hair curling wetly on his muscular chest. He dropped to the sand next to her. Instinctively she scooted over, needing more space. Christos gave her a peculiar look. "Nervous?" he asked.

"No!"

"Good. Because we are married, Alysia. This is going to be a real relationship."

Her pained expression didn't go unnoticed. Christos's jaw tightened as he watched her from beneath lowered lashes. Her face was like a canvas, storm after storm crossing the finely drawn features.

He scooped a palm of sand, letting the warm grains trickle between his fingers. "Why did you marry me? What changed your mind?"

Her head jerked up, long blond hair wet, clinging to her slim shoulder. "What?"

"You changed your mind about marrying me. Why?"

She didn't answer and he reached out, opened his palm, trickling the soft sand to fall onto the inside of her arm. Alysia snatched her arm away and the warm grains slid to her inner thigh.

The pale grains of sand on her taut thigh were too irresistible to ignore. He lightly brushed the trail of sand from her thigh. Alysia gasped and jerked her knees closed, trapping his hand. He felt the smooth plane of muscle in her thigh, the heat of her body, the silky satin of her skin.

A faint tremor coursed through her. He felt it ripple through him and glancing at her, he arched one eyebrow. "This is nice."

Pink color darkened her cheeks, a blush of mortification. Her knees opened and she shoved his hand away from her leg.

"I rather liked it there," he drawled.

"Keep your hands to yourself."

"I want a marriage, Alysia. I want you."

"You said you'd give me time."

"I am. I have. But how much more time is necessary? You're attracted to me—"

"You've quite an imagination, Mr. Pateras, if you honestly believe that!" she interrupted, her head lifting, scorn flashing in her dark blue eyes.

He grinned, enjoying the flash and fire in her eyes. He liked it when she was angry, liked the fury and the challenge he saw buried there. "I do have a rather vivid imagination and I've a number of ideas I'd like to try with you."

"I might not be a virgin, Mr. Pateras, but I'm afraid I lack your level of sexual expertise. You might be better off finding a partner that could better satisfy your needs."

"I don't want a mistress. I want you."

"*No.*"

"Why can't I want you?"

"Because you don't even know me." She dug her hands into the sand, burying her skin to the wrist. "And you can't want someone you've only just met."

"Why not?"

"Because. It's just not right."

"Ah, your morals. I see. You'll marry a man to escape your father but you won't stoop low enough to want him."

"No, that's not it."

"That's exactly it. You'd find it a whole lot easier to accept our arrangement if you were forced to endure my touch, then you could blame it on me. But the truth is, you want my touch and that makes you angry.''

Alysia jumped to her feet and began brushing the sand from the back of her legs with tangible violence. "I'm not attracted to you, I don't want you and I want nothing to do with you."

"Little late for that, don't you think?"

Suddenly she stiffened, and raised a hand to shield her eyes as she stared out toward the water. Her lips parted in a silent oh, her focus entirely fixed on the tide. He felt her tension, her slender body taut, her breath bottled. She stood like that another couple of seconds before running frantically to the water's edge.

Alysia saw the small body floating face down, arms outstretched, legs apart. She heard a scream, someone was screaming and she lunged into the water, grabbing at the child, flipping him up.

Breathe, she shouted, breathe.

The little boy wiggled, blue rubber mask framing his dark startled eyes. The sea-green snorkel fell from between his clenched baby teeth.

He wasn't dead. He was swimming. Snorkeling.

Her legs turned to jelly and she nearly collapsed into the water, still clutching the little boy to her chest.

People surged towards her. Women, men, the other children, everyone yelling at once.

"Down," the little boy imperiously demanded, no longer frightened, just angry. "Put me down now."

Above the commotion she caught Christos's gaze,

his dark eyes fixed on her. There was no anger in his eyes, no expression at all. Weakly she set the child down, placing him on his feet.

A woman, his mother most likely, yanked him into her arms, turning on Alysia in a tirade of angry Greek. Alysia saw the woman's mouth move, flapping, flapping, flapping, but heard nothing the mother said, her brain dazzled by silence, stunned to stillness by the wretched memory of death.

Christos worked through the crowd, circling her shoulders with one arm, pushing the others away. "Shall we go?"

She nodded, her brain dimly aware of the pressure of his arm around her body, his size shielding her from the others nearby.

Her mouth felt parched, dry like the sand. They walked across the beach, leaving the others behind. Christos stopped briefly, bending over to gather their towels and shirts.

At the boat he undid the knotted rope. She waded to the boat, water surging around her thighs, swirling to her hips. She climbed up the boat's ladder and moved toward the driver's seat.

Christos glanced at her as the speedboat sliced through the ocean on the way back to the yacht, but he said nothing, and for that, she was grateful.

She couldn't look at him, couldn't talk to him, too mired in grief. Her stomach cramped, pain contorting in her belly. She clutched her hair in one hand and hunched over the side of the Donzi, throwing up into the saltwater.

Alexi.

Christos had seen the look on her face as she'd pulled the little boy up, snorkel, mask and all, it was a look of dread and terror, the expression of one who has seen a ghost.

Toweling off after his shower, Christos quickly dressed, donning black trousers and a fine white dress shirt.

She hadn't wanted to talk about what happened on the beach and he hadn't pressed for an explanation. It was enough that they both knew she'd run for the boy, seeing something else, thinking something else.

Christos saw enough today to feel worry of his own. Alysia's ghost would haunt her forever if he didn't try to help. He had to do something. But what?

He slid his arms into his black tuxedo jacket, grateful they'd be dining out tonight. They were dining on Cephalonia tonight, joining Christos's closest friends at Constantine Pappas's elegant villa, and he thought the party atmosphere would be good for Alysia, especially in light of what happened on the beach today.

He'd told her that dress for dinner was formal and while knotting his tie, Christos found himself wondering what she'd wear.

He imagined the long gowns she might pick from, beaded fabrics, velvet fabrics, delicate silk fabrics, but nothing he thought, could be more seductive than the conservative two-piece swimsuit she'd worn at the beach today.

Her suit, a pale pink tank-style with thin spaghetti straps, clung to her breasts and hips like a second skin. And wet, the fabric revealed the contours of her nipple, the cleft in her derriere, the protruding hipbones. He'd wanted to take her right there in the warm sand, pull her down beneath him and bury himself inside her.

Jutting his jaw to better see his collar, Christos knotted his black bow tie, then snapped off the bathroom light. Time to check on his bride.

CHAPTER FIVE

"You didn't tell me we were joining other shipowners for dinner!" Alysia stared at Christos in dismay, her thin silk shawl folded over her arm, her small beaded purse clutched in her fingers. She'd imagined a quiet dinner alone with Christos. Instead they'd be spending the evening with old, powerful Greek families, families that knew too much of her family history.

"I thought I'd mentioned it."

"No, you did not."

He inclined his head, his black hair gleaming like polished onyx, his white shirt a perfect foil for his dark, hard features. "I apologize, then. It must have slipped my mind. We've been invited to Constantine Pappas's for dinner. You know him, I believe?"

Oh, she knew Constantine Pappas very well. Not only had he once been her father's best friend, but he'd created tremendous, and lasting, controversy in the Greek shipping industry by inviting foreigners to invest in his company, investors like Christos.

Suddenly it dawned on her, that Christos might very well be Constantine's silent foreign investor. "You're not...you don't...with Mr. Pappas?"

"Are you asking if I'm his business partner? The

answer is yes. I've backed his business for nearly ten years.''

"Constantine and my father are enemies." But she saw from Christos's expression he already knew that. "But my father doesn't know that, does he?"

"No. I've always been a silent investor. And I've had my own business. Your father only knows me as an American holding company."

"He doesn't really know you, does he?"

"We're business acquaintances. Not friends."

She felt a bubble of hysteria. "So how did you make the deal? Did he ask to see your stock portfolio? Your savings accounts, what?"

"I sent him some income tax statements."

"Income tax statements. Amazing. You had money, he had a daughter, a deal was struck." Shock made her tongue thick. Tears welled in her eyes. "How many men did he go through trying to find one rich enough?"

"I don't know, Alysia, it doesn't really matter anymore, does it?"

"Not to you, because you won. You got Lemos's name, Lemos's ships, Lemos's business and Lemos's daughter." The shame of it made her skin crawl. What kind of man sold off his only child? What kind of man would sell her to a virtual stranger? Christos wasn't even Greek. He was American. He was everything her father despised and yet it didn't matter because Christos was rich, filthy rich, appallingly rich.

"I hate you!" She swung her beaded purse, swiping him in the chest. "I hate that you'd do this to me. To *us*."

The moment she'd said "us" she'd realized why she felt so crazy the past few days. If she'd met Christos anywhere else, in any other situation, she would have fallen in love with him, fallen for his impossible good looks, his strength, his sensuality. Instead marrying him like this destroyed everything. He was a mercenary and all the charm in the world couldn't change that one horrible fact.

"I'm sorry." There was no emotion in his deep voice, nothing at all.

"I'm not going with you tonight," she said, blinking away the tears, her chest tender, her throat sore. "If you want to celebrate your victory, you go without me."

"Constantine is throwing the party for us. It'd be a slap in his face to not show up."

"I can't go there. I can't face everyone."

"Why not? Because you feel like an outsider? Guess what, darling, I've spent my life on the outside. I know what it's like to be the subject of constant speculation. I've heard the criticism about my past. But I don't care what others think. I don't need to please anyone but myself."

"Obviously," she flung back. He might consider himself Greek, but he was still an American. He'd been born in another country, raised with another society's values. As much as he wanted to think of himself as Greek, he was still alien, would always remain alien, despite his marriage to her. "I'm not going tonight. I want no part of this. You've made your deal with my father. Now leave me alone.''

He shrugged, unmoved. ''You made a deal with me, too, and I expect you to hold up your end of the bargain.''

''It's not a fair bargain!''

''You should have thought about it earlier. But since you are a Pateras now, you shall do I as ask.''

''Ask?''

''Insist.'' His dark eyes narrowed, his jaw jutting harshly, hinting at emotions he so far hadn't revealed. ''As my wife you will go with me tonight and treat Constantine Pappas with respect, indeed, reverence. Is that clear?''

The yacht slowly motored into the harbor, pulling up alongside the dock. Alysia and Christos didn't speak as they stepped ashore, and the silence continued once they were seated in the waiting Rolls-Royce.

In the car Alysia wondered how much Christos actually knew about her father's relationship with Constantine. The two had once been best friends, growing up together on Oinoussai and attending college together. It wasn't until they'd both gone to work in the shipping industry that their friendship changed. Always competitive, they grew suspicious of the other. Suddenly a lifelong friendship turned into a bitter rivalry, exploding one summer into wild accusations of cheating, stealing, lying, and petty crime.

The chauffeured car pulled up in front of

Constantine's enormous villa, the white marble building glimmering with light, and Alysia brought herself to speak. "Mr. Pappas must be shocked by our marriage."

"Everyone's a bit intrigued," he answered.

And that was putting it mildly, she suspected. Alysia gripped her pale blue silk shawl and drew the fringed edges to her breast, her dress the color of aquamarine. "People will gossip."

"They do anyway."

"Yet everyone knows he was trying to find a husband for me. He'd practically advertised in all the Greek papers!"

Christos's white teeth gleamed in the darkness. "You forget, everyone believes ours is a love match. We had a secret wedding. Most people will assume we've gone behind your father's back."

"My reputation."

"Is in tatters," he agreed, reaching out to touch the slender sapphire-and-diamond bracelet encircling her wrist.

The chauffeur swung the back door of the Rolls-Royce open and stepped back, silently attentive.

But Alysia couldn't bring herself to move. She felt tricked somehow, outwitted into this game. All her life she'd been manipulated by her father and now she was married to a man who intended to do the same. A lump formed in her throat. "I thought you might have been different."

Christos's jaw tightened, a small muscle popping. He ignored the chauffeur, his full attention on her.

"Sometimes we have to bend the rules to get ahead."

"Bend the rules? You mean, break them, don't you? You play every bit as underhanded as my father."

She felt the weight of his gaze. "Perhaps, but my motives are different."

"So you say!"

"I guess you'll just have to trust me."

"Trust you?" Slowly she shook her head, disbelief coloring her speech. "I'd trust my father before I trusted you. At least I've known him all my life. You, I just met."

Christos's large, callused palm clasped her clenched fists, gathering them into his hands. He kissed her clenched fists and then released them. "Sometimes strangers can be blessings in disguise. Now come, it's time we went inside."

Alysia had to admit that Constantine was a better host than her father would have been. He greeted her warmly, kissing her on both cheeks, congratulating her on her marriage. If he felt acrimonious toward her, there was no sign of it. She found herself struggling, though, to answer his polite inquiries about her father with equal enmity. Clearly Constantine sought to put past tensions behind them. She could do no less.

"Well done," Christos whispered into her ear, as they moved from Constantine and his wife to another couple.

She tried to hold herself aloof as Christos discussed business with the other man, but he snaked an arm around her waist and drew her firmly against his side. His fingers kneaded softly into her waist, moving down slightly to caress her hip.

Alysia attempted to draw away, and his arm only tightened, holding her more firmly. An escape was impossible.

Throwing her head back, she parted her lips to protest but caught the warning light in his eyes. Remember where you are, his expression said, remember who we're with.

Men. Businessmen. And Christos was conducting business.

She swallowed the bitterness in her mouth, unwillingly flashing back to a time she'd impulsively interrupted one of her father's meetings to ask if she could join a group of teenagers heading to an Athens disco. She'd never been to a disco, never been dancing. It had sounded exciting and despite her mother's warning, she'd gone to her father, desperate for permission. Her mother had been right. Her father was furious at the interruption, slapping her sharply across the face in front of a dozen men. He'd slapped her and sent her to bed.

Instead of dancing she'd wept for hours, trapped in her loneliness, and her shame.

Her father had crushed her feeble attempts at independence, refusing to permit her even the smallest of freedoms, wanting the traditional Greek daughter.

The slow circle of Christos's thumb against her hipbone permeated the cloud of memory and with a small jolt, her attention returned to the business discussion and the warmth of Christos's hand on her hip.

Heat shimmered within her, a spark of awareness that made her tingle from head to toe. And again she felt desire stir, languorous need awakening, threatening to possess her rational mind.

As Christos and the other man discussed the European market and the American economy, Alysia's head began to swim, dazed by the tension flooding her limbs. As the conversation continued, she heard fewer words, too aware of the blood surging through her, the tightening in her belly making her thoughts race in a dangerous direction. She'd never felt desire like this. It made her desperate to answer the emptiness aching inside her.

Just when she thought she couldn't stand it anymore, the couple moved on and she caught his fingers in one hand, lifting them from her hip.

"Don't," she gritted, undone by the intimacy, overwhelmed by her hungry response.

"We're supposed to be happy. We're newlyweds in love."

She stiffened in silent protest, hating how powerless she felt, helpless with needs she couldn't control. If he could make her feel this way in public, what would happen tonight when they were alone?

She couldn't let him make love to her. She wasn't on birth control, she doubted he'd wear a condom. He'd made it clear that he wanted children and he wanted them soon. One of these nights he'd push to consummate the marriage. Maybe even tonight.

She had to leave, couldn't afford to wait for another opportunity.

She had to go. Immediately. The party was the perfect cover. So many beautiful people coming and going, music playing, a hum of activity. Christos wouldn't even know she'd gone until too late.

Afraid she'd lose her resolve, she turned to him, murmured an excuse, a pretense of needing to use the ladies' room. Quickly she moved away, out of the white-and-gold ballroom, down the hall, continuing to a narrower passage, one that cut through to the kitchen.

She ignored the kitchen staff, her head high, her purse dangling carelessly from her wrist. She didn't run. Just kept her gaze fixed on the door before her.

The driveway, lined with a dozen expensive imported cars, Bentleys and Rolls-Royces, Mercedes, Jaguars and Ferraris, looked like an exotic car show. Alysia passed the parked cars with barely a glance, nodding briefly at the cluster of drivers who stood in front of a marble lion smoking.

One driver—her driver?—called out to her, asking if she needed a ride. She shook her head and continued on, knowing that a taxi would be the safest option.

She flagged the taxi, a four-person Mercedes, not far from the Trapano Bridge at the south end of Argostoli. Close to the harbor, she could smell the pungent salt in the air, and the hum of the ocean.

"Where to?" the driver asked.

"Sami," she said, directing him to the island's other port, a small village with ferry access to other islands, as well as the mainland. And Sami lay miles from bustling Argostoli with its community of wealthy shipowners who knew too much about her and the Lemos family. No one in Sami would know her.

Alysia pawned her diamond-and-sapphire bracelet in Sami for necessary cash. Out of the money she'd gotten for the bracelet she paid for her ferry ride to Lefkas, and then on Lefkas, was able to buy a one-way plane ticket on Olympic Airways for Athens.

How ironic, she thought with a small twist of her lips, that the bracelet, a gift from her father on her sixteenth birthday, should now buy her freedom.

If only she'd taken the bracelet to Paris, pawned it there. She could have used the money. It might have saved Alexi.

Suddenly she saw Alexi's perfect face, his silvery blond curls, his small arms outstretched, floating.

Floating.

Alysia squeezed her eyes shut, pressed her knuckles against her mouth and fought to erase the memory. For a long moment she sat hunched, her insides frozen, her body rigid with endless, wordless grief.

To think that a bracelet could save her baby's life.

To think that a bracelet could have saved her sanity.

But, no, she couldn't think like that. She'd promised her mother she wouldn't think like that. Those thoughts were the dark ones that ate her alive. Those thoughts nearly destroyed her before. She had to live in the moment. There was only the moment. The past was gone. And the future lay ahead.

In Athens she called an old childhood friend, Lalia, to see if she couldn't perhaps stay with her for a few days until she arranged for a new passport.

Lalia, who'd always been very modern, so far forgoing marriage to pursue a career as a textile designer, was more than happy to accommodate Alysia, especially as she was preparing to fly to London on business and was anxious to find a housesitter for her high-strung cat.

"Zita's very sensitive and he hates disruption," Lalia said, gathering her travel bags and taxi fare together. "Don't be disappointed if he won't play. He'll probably hide until I come home. Just feed him and pretend everything's normal."

Alysia checked her smile. "How like a man."

"Speaking of men, I thought you were married?"

"Rumors." Alysia held the door open for her friend. "Now go, before you miss your flight. And don't worry about a thing. Zita and I will get along just fine."

The first day alone Alysia did nothing but sleep, and read, and sleep some more. The second day she made some calls. The government office handling passports couldn't help her without a copy of her birth certificate, which would require her coming into the office in person to fill out the necessary paperwork.

She hung up the phone and reluctantly conceded that she'd have to visit the government building in person. She'd hoped to avoid going out in public but perhaps if she donned a hat and sunglasses she'd pass unrecognized.

Zita, the onyx-colored, tailless cat, poked his head out from beneath the lace curtains at the window and gazed at her through narrowed eyes.

Alysia imagined she saw disapproval in Zita's slitted eyes and turned her back on the cat. Everything's fine, she firmly told herself. Don't let a cat put your nerves on edge.

The labyrinth of government offices exercised Alysia's strained patience. An afternoon spent waiting in long lines, filling out paperwork in duplicate, only to be sent to another endless line, turned a beautiful autumn afternoon into sheer torture.

Three hours after entering the government building, Alysia left, having been informed that the passport, even if rushed, would take two weeks to process.

Two weeks.

Alysia let herself into Lalia's apartment. Closing the door with one hand, she kicked off her leather loafers and dropped her purse on top of the shoes.

Barefoot she padded down the hall and into the kitchen, opening the refrigerator door for a bottle of chilled mineral water. "Zita," she called. "Hungry?"

The cat didn't answer. Of course, she hadn't expected it to answer, but people were supposed to take to their cats, right?

With her bottle of water in hand she headed toward the living room, richly patterned rugs—all Lalia's design—beneath her bare feet. "Zita! Where are you? Still hiding?"

She stopped short. A man, a tall, broad-shouldered man, sat on the sofa—no, dominated the sofa—with a tailless black cat curled in his lap.

Christos.

CHAPTER SIX

"HELLO, Mrs. Pateras," Christos said, his tone disarmingly conversational as he caressed Zita's dark head. "How was your day?"

She stared at the broad tanned hand cupped over the cat's head, strong fingers slowly, deliberately scratching behind Zita's short, pointy ears, and began to tremble. Her legs suddenly went nerveless, turning into mush.

The bottle of water almost slid from her fingers. "Christos."

"You remembered," he retorted with a savage twist of his lips. He rose so swiftly from the couch that he nearly dumped Zita on his feet. "I wasn't sure if you would. But then, I'm only your *husband*."

He smiled at her, and yet there was nothing remotely kind in his expression, his features granite-like, his dark eyes glittering.

Zita meowed a protest at being so unceremoniously dumped from his comfortable resting place, but Christos ignored the cat, and clenching his fists, took a quick step toward her before checking himself.

She felt his anger, his barely controlled temper, and a sick tremor coursed through her. "Ahh…"

"What was that, sweetheart? Cat got your tongue?"

His joke went in one ear and out the other. She couldn't speak, her tongue wooden, her jaw taut, fear turning her inside out. Instead she helplessly shook her head, her gaze darting to the door and then back at Christos.

"I wouldn't try it. You won't get away and you'll only make me angry."

"And you're not angry now?" she flashed, finding her voice, and simultaneously stunned by the weakness in her knees. She felt as if her legs would buckle beneath her any moment now.

"Oh, I'm angry all right, I'm fit to be tied. But my father has persuaded me to show you mercy."

Mercy. What an odd, terrifying, and yet incredibly Greek thing to say.

Christos moved toward her, closing the distance between them. She was forced to tilt her head back to see his face, realizing belatedly she'd forgotten his height, and the sheer size of him.

"How did you find me?"

"You didn't think I would?" A black eyebrow lifted, expressing surprise.

"You didn't know I was on the mainland. You don't know Lilia."

"But I know you." His eyes gleamed, dark and hard, fixing on her face with predatory instinct. His smile deepened and it was the coldest, most malevolent smile she'd ever seen. "I knew you'd apply for a passport. I knew you'd try to leave Greece."

Her tongue thick and heavy, wouldn't form words. Instead she stared at him, dry-mouthed, wide-eyed, unable to think a single coherent thought. Fear pummeled her brain, melted her bones. "No..." she whispered helplessly. "It couldn't have been so easy."

"Sweetheart, it was too easy. Like taking candy from a baby." He stopped in front of her, reached out and lifted one gold strand from her shoulder, sliding the tendril through his fingers as if silk. "You see, sweet Alysia, I have a home here in Athens. I spend a great deal of time here. New York may be my headquarters, but I maintain offices in Athens, too. I have employees in Athens, and they've been watching you, from the moment you flew into the airport to the moment you just walked in the door."

Horror filled her. He'd had her followed the past few days. She'd been under surveillance. A prisoner, his prisoner, and she didn't even know it.

Slowly he coiled the tendril around his finger, wrapping it into a honey ribbon. He wrapped it tighter then gave a little pull, making her wince.

"You made a fool out of me," he murmured with another small tug. "In front of my colleagues and friends. You humiliated me at the Pappas's, created quite a stir. You should be punished. How shall I punish you? Any suggestions?"

Her tongue continued to cleave to the roof of her mouth. Her heart hammered. "No."

One of Christos's thick black brows lifted. "No suggestions, or no to punishment?"

All this time she thought—believed—she was free. These past several days had felt like heaven. Instead she'd been his, remained his possession. It made her want to weep with frustration. "Why did you think I'd want to leave Greece?"

"You hate Greece. You feel trapped here. I imagine you wanted to fly to England, look up your mother's family." Carefully he unwound the tendril.

"You're awfully clever, aren't you?"

"No. You're just awfully predictable."

"Go to hell!"

Almost absently he caressed her cheek. "Don't be childish, Alysia. It's not becoming."

She flinched at his touch, drawing sharply away. "I can't believe you had me followed."

"How could you think I wouldn't protect my investment?"

The softness in his voice, the husky tone, contrasted cruelly with his expression. His eyes said it all. She'd betrayed him.

He reached into a pocket and withdrew the diamond-and-sapphire bracelet she'd recently pawned. "Here. Put it back on."

She cringed at the bracelet, hating the reminder of the power Christos held over her. "No."

"Do it. Or I will." Without waiting for her to answer he took her hand, flipped her wrist open and snapped the glittering bangle onto her slender arm.

It looked completely incongruous with her leather loafers and casual clothes yet it felt heavy, like iron, he was shackling her to him, taking control of her life again.

"Do not take it off," he said curtly, "and do not think of running away again."

"I refuse to be an object, Christos!"

"You're no object. You're my wife." He tilted her chin up with one of his fingers, his dark eyes searching her mutinous expression. "I erred in judgment once, but I won't make the same mistake again. It's time I exerted my rights in this marriage and time you behaved like a proper Greek wife."

She knew, a split second in advance, that he was going to kiss her. Yet there was no escaping him. His mouth crushed hers, grinding her lips apart, his tongue boldly thrusting inside her mouth, stabbing at the softness with ill-concealed contempt.

But even as his tongue lashed at her sensitive contours, her body warmed, her innermost muscles tightening in anticipation. Despite everything, she wanted him.

Christos's dark head lifted and he gazed into her eyes, a mocking smile etched on his lips. "I'm beginning to understand why your father found it necessary to keep you locked up. You're wild. You're utterly wanton."

Heat burned in bands across the tops of her cheekbones. She tried to take a step back but his hands clasped her at the waist, fingers dipping into the small of her spine.

Again his mouth crushed hers, his tongue raking the sensitive contours of her mouth, thrusting at the hollow of her cheek, beneath her tongue, even tracing the roof of her mouth.

She clung to him, clasping his arms, her legs without strength. She felt mindless with wanting and helplessly opened her mouth wider to him, her tongue finding his, teasing.

He moved to strip her of her jeans, but his hand stilled on her tummy. "Stop me, now—" he muttered thickly, but she didn't speak, and she didn't answer him.

With a groan he tugged her jeans down and then her panties, pulling them off her ankles and casting them to the ground. She felt him grind his hips against hers, his erection creating friction between her thighs.

He worked his zipper down, dropped his own trousers even as his fingers slid between her legs, finding her heat and to her shame, her eager moisture.

Christos dropped her to the ground and parted her legs with his knees. He held her bottom in his hands and without a word, drove into her.

She gasped at the thrust, her body forced to accommodate his size, and she buried her knuckles into his back, overwhelmed by the intensity of his body filling hers, joining them intimately together.

He shifted, easing slowly out of her and then with a kiss on her neck, entered her again, filling her once more, making stars sputter against her tightly closed eyes.

And he made love to her without a word, without

another kiss, just moving inside her slowly, deeply to pull out and enter again, and again, and again.

He felt long, hard, thick, and yet his skin was as smooth as silk, his hips hard and narrow, in her hands. She clung to him as he moved inside her, scarcely daring to breathe, caught up in the pictures he was painting in her head. Him, her, the constellation of stars.

She felt him tense, a soft groan coming from his lips, and as he surged forward, deeper into her, she felt herself step out into the darkest night and fall, silently, blindly into waves of sensation. She rode the waves with desperation, clasping Christos's shoulders, burying her face against his broad chest.

There was no one but them. No place but now. Nothing but this.

Him, her, his body still straining, his hands now cradling her head.

She'd never come before. Never had an orgasm.

"I'm sorry," Christos said thickly, untangling his limbs, his skin still damp, his black hair disheveled. He drew away, rubbed his face with one hand, stood up.

He was sorry and he was done. So that's how he felt. It wasn't what she'd imagined, wasn't what she'd experienced. Nothing beautiful for him. Just a physical act. A form of exercise.

She sat up slowly, realizing they both still wore their shirts but not pants.

Thank goodness she'd just had her period. Thank

God she shouldn't be fertile now. She couldn't, wouldn't, conceive.

He stepped into his underwear and then his pants. "Did I hurt you?" he demanded, his voice pitched low, almost rough.

"No." She wanted to tell him it had been incredible, that even without love, it was the most sensual experience of her life. She'd answered each of his thrusts by lifting her own hips, wrapped her arms around his neck to draw him even closer, wanting it all, wanting him. But now…no pants, the dampness of him inside her, the obvious disgust on his face…

Good thing there was no love between them, no love lost, either.

What had they done? What had she been thinking?

Christos raked a hand through his dark hair, attempting to comb it into submission. "Dress. It's time to go. My driver is downstairs waiting."

He didn't speak on the short drive home. He felt Alysia's revulsion. It mirrored his own.

He was appalled by his actions, stunned that he'd forced himself on her. He'd taken her without regard to her feelings, or her needs.

Christos was grateful when the limousine drew in front of his estate, the palatial marble villa rising from behind iron gates and exotic greenery.

The gates magically slid open and the car continued up the driveway, the powerful engine vibrating like a great beast. He couldn't wait to get out of the car and as far from Alysia's accusing eyes as possible.

He'd promised to respect her, promised to never force himself on her, and yet what did he do but throw her onto the ground and bury himself inside her?

Alysia cast a desperate glance behind her at the high wrought-iron fence and gatehouse before turning to face the dozen employees gathered on the villa's front steps.

Christos nodded at them and then gestured toward Alysia, his expression grim. "The wife," he announced curtly, before continuing up the sweeping circular staircase, leaving her to follow like a child in disgrace.

She flushed, and wordlessly trailed after him, aware of the cool scrutiny of his employees.

Reaching the top of the stairs Christos showed her into a lofty room that was obviously his own private quarters. Desk, leather armchairs, reading lamps.

He closed the door, motioned her to one of the leather chairs. She sat gingerly on the edge of one, wondering what would come next.

"I'm sorry I lost my temper. I behaved like a brute. It won't happen like that again." His speech was sharp, and short. He leaned against the shut door, his arms crossing over his chest, muscles tight, tension emanating from him in great silent waves. "Your father warned me you'd try to run away. He said you'd go the first chance you got. I thought I was prepared. Yet I let down my guard at the party."

She squirmed inwardly realizing how humiliated he must have been at Constantine's. Everyone looking for her. Everyone aware that his new bride had deserted him.

"Your father called," he continued. "He offered his services, apologized for your behavior."

She ducked her head, even more mortified. Her father calling to offer *his* services!

"I told him no thank you, of course." Christos's dark gaze met hers, his expression flinty. "I said you'd be back in no time and soon fulfilling your duty, providing me with sons."

Her heart beat faster. Her throat threatened to seal close. And still she didn't speak so he plunged on. "We will make love until you conceive. We will start that family. You will prove to your father—and the other Greek ship owners—that my faith in you isn't misplaced, that you know and accept your responsibility."

"No."

Her voice was but a whisper and yet he heard it. "No what, Alysia?"

"No, I will not give you children." She lifted her head, looked him in the eye. "No sons. Not even daughters. No heirs."

"Is this a philosophical issue for you? Part of your rebellion against Greek society?"

"A personal issue."

"Ah, then we can work through this."

"No, we can't work through this. You married the wrong woman. You chose the wrong wife. A hundred women could have filled my position. A hundred women would have begged to bear your children. I, on the other hand, will not.''

His smile had all but disappeared and she slid instinctively backward, hips hugging the chair, even though he hadn't moved from the door. ''I have tried to be patient, Alysia, tried to understand your feelings, but my patience is about gone. We need to move forward. We need to start our future.''

He approached her quietly, crouching at her feet, his palms sliding up her shins, over her knees, electrifying her legs. Awareness exploded in her middle, tension coiling in her lower belly making her thighs tremble.

Christos's dark gaze momentarily met hers and he smiled—if the slight twist of lips could be called a smile—acknowledging her unwilling response.

His palm shaped her outer thigh and followed with his body. She felt the press of his chest against her knees as he parted them, moving between her legs.

Blood pumped through her veins, heat searing her face, shredding countless nerve endings beneath her skin. It shocked her that she could still want him, shocked her that she could feel so raw and physical even after what had taken place at Lilia's apartment.

''Not again,'' she gritted as his thumbs caressed the lean line of her thigh.

''And just what do you think I'm going to do?'' he drawled, his voice never more husky, never more American than now.

Her mouth felt so dry that it cleaved to the roof of her mouth. She stared into his face, drowning in sensation, painfully aware of the size distinction between them.

"You're going to want more...sex," she retorted, her voice more breathy than angry, her body so traitorously warm she despised herself.

"I'll take more time, this time, I'll take it slow." He dropped a fleeting kiss against the side of her neck, just beneath her earlobe.

She tried to kick him again. He held her tighter. "You are the worst kind of man."

"The worst kind? Lower than your father?" He pressed another equally brief, equally tantalizing kiss to the outline of her breast, just brushing the taut, aching nipple. "That is a shame."

Warmth surged through her, traitorous warmth and she wanted to weep with frustration. She couldn't believe she'd want a man she hated so much, and yet her body, her stupid wretched, needy body was responding to him in hungry, wanton desperation.

His lips found her nipple again, closing around the exquisitely sensitive bud, suckling it through her blouse. She squirmed helplessly, fire and need rolling through her in great waves. For a half second she clung to him, closing her eyes and giving herself over to the pleasure of desire. She allowed herself to feel it all—the throb of his muscular body, the heat simmering beneath her skin, the insistent need between her thighs—and then when the craving became too strong, she wrenched away, rolling out from beneath Christos's arm to stand across the room, facing the window.

"You don't like me, I understand that," he said quietly, his voice devoid of all emotion, "but we're married. We have to make this work."

She squeezed her eyes closed as if to shut out his voice. "You will never get what you want from me."

He rose, yet he didn't leave. She felt his presence as if he still held her in his arms. "I don't know what happened between you and your first husband, but Jeremy Winston did something to you—"

"No."

"He put a curse on you, froze your heart, trapping you like Sleeping Beauty in the tower."

"You don't know what you're talking about."

"I know enough. I know your marriage ended with heartbreak. I know you spent nearly two years in Switzerland, after you left the Sanatorium, trying to find yourself again."

Alysia's head felt light, so light that it tingled at the top. "I can't talk about it."

"Why not? What happened, Alysia?"

"Nothing happened."

"Something did—"

"No!"

"Something so dark, so terrible—"

The words surged around her, words sweeping, blurring until the room spun with words and she heard nothing more.

Christos had called a doctor and the doctor, after a thorough exam, recommended rest, vitamins and more iron. Women, the doctor said, are often anemic and if they wanted to conceive, it would be wise for Alysia to increase her iron intake.

"I'm not that anemic," she protested, a day after the doctor had been called, and facing her third steak in a row. "I can get iron from spinach. I don't have to eat a platter of steaks."

"We can't have babies if you're not strong."

"I am strong, and I don't have to gorge on meat to conceive. Now back off with the bully routine. I won't be intimidated."

Christos visibly fought to control his temper. "I'm not trying to intimidate you. I just want you to be careful."

"I am careful. I'm also bored. I'd like to get some fresh air. If that's all right with you, of course."

He muttered something beneath his breath and shook his head, obviously eager to end the discussion. "You may go to the pool. I'll have the maid put towels on a lounge chair for you. But don't stay out in the sun too long. You don't want to burn."

Alysia dragged the chaise lounge from beneath the umbrella closer to the pool where she could enjoy the sparkle of the sun on the clear, aquamarine water. She'd brought a book downstairs with her but it turned out to be a rather dry historical account requiring more concentration than she could muster at the moment. After a half hour of reading, she tossed the hardback aside and gave herself over to the pleasure of nothing.

The sun felt wonderful on her back and unhooking the bikini top, she wiggled into the towel, drinking in the steady warm sunshine and promptly fell asleep.

Sometime later, she had no idea how long, she felt a touch, a lovely caress, like feathers or velvet dragged gently across her bare spine.

Sighing she nestled into the towel, not wanting to lose the delicious sensation. The leisurely caress repeated itself, and her lower tummy tightened, warming. She breathed in slowly, not wanting to open her eyes and lose the dreamy sensation.

The velvetlike touch played at the edge of her bikini bottoms, lingering over the line of skin just above the patch of fabric. She wiggled a little, teased by the touch and yet disappointed by the brevity.

Suddenly it clasped her bottom, no tentative touch, but a large hand firmly cupping the curve of cheek.

This was no dream.

Alysia leaped up, snatching her bikini top even as she struggled to cover herself. "Christos!"

The tall shadow shifted, creating a sliver of sunlight where darkness had been. He sat down on the lounge chair next to her. "You should have put lotion on. You've been out here hours and burned yourself to a crisp."

She glanced at her wrist, no watch, and then up at the sun. It had moved. A great deal, actually. A quarter of the way through the sky. "What time is it?" she demanded, struggling to get her bikini top back on without exposing herself.

"Quarter to four."

"*What?*"

He watched her fumble with the flimsy fabric with interest. "Perhaps I should help you."

"I don't need your help."

"You need to put something on the burn. You don't want the skin to blister."

"It's never blistered before." Yet her trembling fingers made it almost impossible to adjust the scrap of fabric across her chest. She had a horrible sensation that one nipple, or the other, would pop out at any moment.

"Alysia, I have seen breasts before."

"But never mine."

His lip curled, a black eyebrow winged. Laughter tinged his husky voice. "I'm sure I can handle the shock."

Of course he'd say something smart like that. He was a born wit. Jumping to her feet, she grabbed her towel and slid into her robe with just the briefest flash of flesh. "Unfortunately I don't think I can."

The silk robe felt ice-cold against her hot back and she winced as she tied the silk sash around her waist. "What time is dinner?"

"Drinks at seven. Dinner at nine."

She'd promised to be there, had planned on meeting him, but Alysia hadn't counted on the extent of her sunburn. It was a livid sunburn.

The warm bath had helped, at first, but as soon as she'd lightly toweled off, her entire backside, from shoulders to her insteps, felt like fire.

She couldn't even pull a pair of panties on without tears starting to her eyes. Her bra straps sliced into her now-blistering shoulders. Nothing in her closet looked comfortable. She stripped off the bra, stripped off the underwear and carefully crawled between cool bed sheets.

To hell with dinner. She'd stay in bed instead.

Too proud to summon Christos, she simply didn't show up downstairs at seven.

Quarter after seven, he arrived at the bedroom door.

He didn't bother to knock. He just walked straight in. "Knowing your penchant for running away, I thought I'd check to see if you were still with us."

Alysia drew the bed sheet toward her chin. "As you can see, I'm still here."

"But in bed."

"Yes."

"Is that, by happy chance, an invitation?" His teeth flashed whitely in a crooked grin.

"No."

"But you appear naked."

"Because I'm too sunburned to dress."

"Show me."

Her stomach did a slow, peculiar curl. Heat prickled across the curve of her cheeks. "You want proof?"

"Please."

CHAPTER SEVEN

PRICKLES of awareness touched her spine, contrasting with the fever raging in her skin. Alysia struggled to deny the feeling. "I'm not going to pull the covers down just so you can see a sunburn."

"You haven't been in the sun for over a year. You could have second- or third-degree burns."

"You're exaggerating. I might be a little sore, but it's just a sunburn."

"I'll be the judge of that." Christos stalked to the edge of the bed and wrenched the covers from her clenched fingers, peeling the sheet back.

Alysia rolled over onto her stomach to protect her front, humiliated by his impersonal scrutiny. "Just a sunburn," she gritted, "I told you. Now will you please allow me some privacy!"

"You're fried to a crisp," he answered, touching the middle of her back.

She couldn't help wincing. It hurt, badly. "*Please*. The covers."

"Not until I put something on your skin first. I've some aloe gel with a topical anesthetic in it that should help."

"Can you at least let me cover my...bottom." She felt his gaze move to the aforementioned and she blushed from head to toe, acutely embarrassed.

"You are modest," he drawled, heading to the bathroom and returning with a hand towel and tube of ointment.

He spread the small towel across her bottom, going to great lengths to adjust it just so, his long fingers brushing the curve of her cheek not just once, but repeatedly, as he slid the small towel up, before tugging it down. To the left. Up a hair. Down a bit, and over to the right.

He was manhandling her and she found it degrading. But that didn't seem to keep her from responding, each brush of his fingers, each slip of the towel sending fiery arcs of feeling through her veins, coiling need in the deepest part of her, a need so strong, so insistent that she throbbed from the inside out.

"That's enough!" she snapped, finding his touch nearly as unbearable as the ache spreading from her womb into her limbs.

His fingers trailed across the dip in her spine, and tugged the small towel higher on her cheek, leaving the underside of her bottom exposed to air. "Are you sure? I wouldn't want to deprive you of your modesty."

"Then perhaps a bigger towel would have been more helpful," she gritted from between clenched teeth.

"I was afraid a bigger towel would irritate the burn."

The cool air seemed to caress her exposed bottom and it took every bit of her self-control to not wiggle.

Part of her felt humiliated and another felt shamelessly excited. "You're the one irritating the burn."

He merely laughed softly, the husky sound reverberating from his chest. Unscrewing the cap from the ointment tube, Christos took a seat next to her on the bed.

His thigh brushed her hip and she tensed, shoulders hunching around her ears. She was aware of Christos in every nerve in her body, feeling his strength and warmth as if he were the sun and she the moon.

He rubbed the aloe between his hands and she could hear the slick lotion slurp against his skin. It struck her as an indecent sound, sexual and raw, and the ache in her lower belly intensified. Pressing her inner thighs together, she tried to control her breathing and yet her heart raced, her senses enflamed. She wanted him to touch her even as she feared it.

"Lie still," he commanded, leaning forward, his sinewy thigh pressing against her own. "This might sting a bit."

Sting? The ointment felt like ice. Helplessly she bucked against his hand, wriggling to escape the prickly hot and cold sensations. But he didn't let her escape. He pressed her down against the sheet and continued applying the aloe gel in slow, steady strokes.

Little by little the anesthetic went to work, numbing the worst of the pain and again making her hopelessly aware of Christos's hands stroking her spine.

His hands moved over her body, down the length of her spinal column, into the dip of her lower back, and then up, over the flare of her hips.

Heat coursed through her, but this warmth had nothing to do with the sunburn and everything to do with his sensuous caress.

His fingertips explored the hollow just above the cleft in her cheeks and she wiggled, telling him to move away. He did, but only to move to her flare of hips, caressing up her waist, to the curve of her breasts.

Alysia couldn't breathe. His thumbs stroked the soft swell. Her nipples hardened, the soft flesh prickling with awareness. She wanted more sensation than feathers and butterflies, more than just this soft teasing touch.

His hands returned to her rib cage and then lifted altogether. She drew a short, shallow breath. ''Thank you,'' she choked.

''Not quite done,'' he answered, lightly massaging her shoulders and nape.

''It's good,'' she replied, her voice sounding thick and slow.

But how could it be otherwise? His touch sent blood coursing through her veins with dizzying speed. She couldn't catch her breath. Her heart raced too fast. Her body quivered from head to toe, but the greatest tension coiled in her middle, hot and heavy, her inner thighs almost dancing with need.

''I haven't covered everything,'' he replied,

squeezing another dollop of gel onto the middle of her back.

She wanted to protest but no sound came from her mouth. Instead she closed her eyes, her lips parting, attuned to every shift of his body, every press of his thigh against her own.

Again his palms fanned the width of her rib cage and curved down to cup her breasts, thumbs flicking across taut, swollen nipples.

Mercy.

If there was purgatory, she'd found it. Caught between heaven and hell and she wanted him to stop just as much as she couldn't let him.

Swept away by touch, sensation, raw physical hunger. Years of being nothing but skin and bones and suddenly she was all nerve endings. Alive, humming, hot liquid desire.

Forget prayers and penance, she'd take sin any day.

He stroked down again, his warm, hard hands moving beneath the towel, shaping the curve of her bottom. The liquid heat between her thighs threatened to consume her. She pressed her legs together tighter, trying to deny the tingle in her flesh, but Christos applied more pressure, deeply kneading the muscles in her bottom and she felt equal waves of shame and craving.

"Don't," she muttered, humiliated and yet sinfully aroused.

"Do you want me to stop?"

"N-n-no." The confession cost her but it was the truth.

Even without being able to see his face, she could feel his smile. But for once she didn't care. The sensations filling her body were too lovely, too consuming to interrupt.

His fingertips discovered the sensitive line between bottom and thigh and he caressed that, too, awakening a river of longing in the only place that hadn't been burned. The teasing of her sensitive flesh created the most awful awareness of her body and needs. She felt huge in that moment, voracious.

She ought to have more control, ought to tell him in scathing tones that she wouldn't put up with such liberties, but oh, liberties had never felt so wonderful. She was quite dizzy with want, and she took in air in short, shallow gasps, afraid to breathe, afraid to distract him, afraid that this pleasure would end.

Pressing her open mouth to her forearm, she shuddered as Christos's fingers slid inward, tracing the cleft of her bottom down, until he'd discovered the tight protective curls and her hot, wanton dampness.

She was on fire, truly, but this had nothing to do with her sunburn and everything to do with need. Suddenly she'd become all liquid and hunger, like molten lava.

No one had ever touched her with such tantalizing intimacy, not even Jeremy who'd been a timid—and dare she admit?—unsatisfying lover. For Jeremy sex had been just that: a brief coupling and then uncoupling. It hadn't crossed her mind to assert that she had physical needs.

When Christos's fingers slid across her slick, sensitive flesh, she trembled, biting her arm to keep from arching against his hand. She couldn't lose control, couldn't betray herself with him. But when he stroked the engorged bud, a thousand nerve endings danced and her hips lifted, as if of their own volition.

He caressed her again, and again, and each time he touched the acutely sensitive bud, she felt as though he was winding her tighter and tighter like an old-fashioned wood top.

More, faster, tighter.

Brilliant color filled her mind, painted stripes of red and green and white against the polished wood.

Stroking her, he wound her tighter still, drawing her in and out of herself, aware of his hands, his warmth, her heat, her labored breathing.

She couldn't catch her breath and the intensity of it made her long to scream. And then when she felt quite mad and mindless, he put her over the edge, setting the coiled wooden top on the ground, fingers stroking faster, faster, faster.

He let her go. And suddenly she was flying, flung across the floor, spinning wildly out of control.

The speed and strength of the climax stunned her. She bit her forearm, choking back a scream, muffling the intensity of her response.

Hell, hell, hell!

She'd thought she'd had an orgasm yesterday, but that…that was nothing like this. This…it was unreal.

Incredible. Unbelievable. One could get addicted to feeling this way.

Her open mouth pressed to her arm drew her back to the moment. Christos stirred and she suddenly remembered him, and his part in this.

He'd brought her to a climax with his hand. Good God, how impersonal. How crude. She longed to bury her face in the pillow and hide but that wouldn't exactly work. He was waiting for her to speak. Waiting for something.

Slowly she turned her head, her eyes feeling heavy, sleepy, and she stared up at Christos. His own gaze looked slumberous, his dark pupils almost black.

He'd enjoyed this, she realized, startled, overwhelmed. He'd enjoying making her fall apart in his hands.

She dampened her bottom lip, overwhelmed by her weakness. And still he waited for her to speak. She grasped at the first thing that came to mind.

"That was nice."

His lashes lowered, concealing his emotions. "I must be out of practice. I'll have to work on that." And with a nod in her direction, he left, leaving her naked and alone in bed.

Sleeping that night was excruciating, her skin so hot she felt as though a fire had been lit beneath her skin. Once she woke to find Christos at her side, aspirin in his hand. She gratefully accepted and allowed him to spray a topical pain relief across her back. He avoided mentioning what had taken place earlier and after he left she fell into a deeper, more restful sleep.

A maid brought a breakfast tray to her in bed and Alysia ate her melon and sweet roll sitting up in bed, moving gingerly, if at all.

Christos appeared briefly, dressed in a suit and tie, dark hair slicked back, accenting the hardness of his features. "How are you feeling?"

"A little better."

"I'd warned you about the sun."

Of course he did. He was the font of all wisdom. She gritted her teeth, resisting the urge to reply sarcastically.

"If you need me, you can reach me at my office."

"I won't need you."

He shrugged. "You say that, but your actions contradict your words." And with that, he was gone.

He was right, she realized, sinking back into bed. She felt completely split, two personalities inhabiting one body. One part of her craved purity, denial, discipline. Another hungered for heat and passion. It'd always been this way, too. As a child she'd felt so emotional, so hungry for affection, and her father's coldness, his critical manner, had made her ashamed of her feelings, turning a little girl's needs into something dirty and wrong.

Daughters were to serve. Daughters were to be silent. Daughters were to sacrifice.

Her father made it clear Alysia failed on all three accounts.

The older she grew, the more she struggled against

her passionate nature, fighting to deny herself, fighting to be what her father demanded of her. She'd always had a knack for drawing and she turned to her giant sketch pads, pouring her energy into endless charcoal drawings, portraits of the family servants, sketches of neighbor children, landscapes of the sea and rocky terrain.

Earning the art scholarship had been an answer to prayer. Her father had been furious that she'd even applied, but her mother somehow persuaded him to let her go. Once in Paris she embraced everything new, relishing the eclectic circle of artists and writers who talked about everything but making money. They were passionate and interesting, clever and original. Jeremy was one of them, always the life of the party, charming, handsome, completely irresponsible. She'd loved that about him. Loved the fact that he couldn't hold a job. Wouldn't hold a job. He was the least controlling person she'd ever known.

They didn't date long. A couple of nights after first making love he suggested they move in together. But deep down she was still a good Greek girl and she couldn't just live with a man. She needed to be a wife, and then a mother.

And so she had been. Both.

Alysia curled on her side, smoothed her hand across the cool cotton sheet. Paris seemed so long ago. Jeremy was just a name of a man she'd once known.

It was strange she thought, she'd lived lives that

didn't exist anymore. The good Greek girl was gone. Only the hedonist remained.

And the hedonist had decided she wanted Christos, wanted to remain with Christos, even if she had to bend the rules to make the relationship work.

He wanted a wife. She'd be his wife. She just wouldn't get pregnant. The doctor had given her a blue plastic case with a six month supply of birth control pills, to give her time to build up her strength before trying for a baby. So for the next six months she was safe. And then she'd see another doctor, and renew the prescription.

Late in the day, Alysia managed to bathe and dress, slipping on a soft cotton sundress and low-heeled sandals. She ate dinner alone in the formal dining room and wandered the garden grounds, hearing the distant horn of a car.

Footsteps sounded on the flagstone path. She turned, discovering Christos behind her. He'd changed from his suit into pale linen trousers and a smooth cotton shirt the color of butterscotch. The caramel color suited him, enhancing his bronze complexion and the gleam of his black hair.

"I'm sorry to have kept you waiting," he said. "There's been a problem at my head office in New York."

He sounded quietly ironic, as if everything between them was a joke. Hurt unfolded inside her chest, hurt because she understood that there was something intrinsically good in him, in them, but they couldn't seem to get around the obstacles.

"I've been all right. I'm quite good at entertaining myself."

He nodded slightly, comprehending her implied reference at learning to stay busy and out of her father's way. "I need to be in New York tomorrow. We'll leave tonight."

She felt a leap of excitement, and a peculiar sense of hope. Cynically she mocked her expectations. Starting over in a new place wasn't exactly starting fresh. The problems would follow. The conflict remained.

But maybe it didn't have to. Perhaps away from Greece they could start over, make something new. Here everything felt tainted. She felt tainted. But in America they could change, she could change. She would try harder. She'd please more.

"I've already instructed Housekeeping to pack. We'll be leaving soon." He hesitated, his expression grim. "There's something else. Your father wanted to stop over tonight, to say goodbye. I told him no. I hope that's all right with you."

Christos's private jet landed so gently that there wasn't even a bump as the plane's wheels touched the tarmac. They taxied to the executive terminal and immediately deplaned, exiting the jet only to be handed into the back of a waiting limousine.

Despite the early hour, dawn just breaking, Christos returned phone calls during the short drive to his country house in Darien, Connecticut.

Once during his conversation, he covered the receiver and leaned forward, pointing out a series land-marks to Alysia.

In the dim morning light it was difficult to see much, but she made out the shapes of ornate iron gates, stone walls and extensive grounds with endless manicured lawns. Although she'd grown up sur-rounded by wealth, the vast American country estates impressed even her.

Christos's house, rather than dominating the ver-dant landscape, nestled into a green knoll as if to take comfort in the undulating land with its views of the water and grove of majestic hardwood trees.

"It's not what you expected," Christos said, not-ing her expression as he hung up the phone.

And it wasn't. She'd expected something grandi-ose, another opulent mansion built of polished mar-ble. Instead this rambling two-story country house had been fashioned from clapboard and stone, fea-turing big beautiful bay windows and discreet cov-ered doorways. The soft morning light outlined the shingled roof, the sharp gables, the cascading roof-line. It was a fairy-tale house, the entry marked by a profusion of climbing roses.

An older woman answered the door, dressed sim-ply in a black jersey dress, her steel-gray hair coiffed in a severe knot. The housekeeper, Alysia assumed. She assumed wrong.

"Mother," Christos said, clasping the woman by the shoulders and kissing both cheeks. "What are you doing up at this hour?"

"I've been waiting by the door."

"So I see."

Alysia went hot, then cold. Not a housekeeper, but his mother. Abruptly the stone and whitewashed clapboard house lost its fairy-tale charm.

Christos made the introductions and his mother, greeted Alysia cordially, if coolly, which didn't surprise Alysia in the slightest. In Greece, mothers-in-law were notoriously hard on daughters-in-law. No woman was ever good enough for another woman's son. Greek mothers lived for their sons and considered it their duty to instruct new wives how to run the household, perform domestic duties.

The elder Mrs. Pateras turned to her son. "She's sick?"

"No, mother, she's just slim."

The gray-haired matron cast a skeptical glance over Alysia's slender figure and wan complexion. "You called a doctor in Athens, no?"

"Yes, Mother, but the doctor assured me she just needs iron. He prescribed some iron tablets and those will help."

Mrs. Pateras's dour expression grew darker. She tossed her hands in the air, gesturing with impassioned emphasis. "I thought you wanted family, Christos. Babies, no? A skinny wife isn't good for making babies. You need a good Greek girl, not a Lemos!"

Alysia expected a mother-in-law who'd been cool, perhaps even critical, but Mrs. Pateras's vocal attack left her speechless, the blood draining from her face, her body cold.

"Mama, gently, please," Christos quietly remonstrated. "You must give Alysia a chance."

"I know all about her. I know she's not the one for you. A good Greek girl, Christos, a *good* girl."

Christos glanced at Alysia, their eyes briefly meeting. "She is a good Greek girl," he answered, his expression blank, his dark eyes shuttered, before turning back to his mother.

"But she's Lemos's daughter."

"Yes."

"So how can she be the right one for you?"

CHAPTER EIGHT

His mother gone, Christos shut the door. "She'll be fine. She just needs time," he said flatly.

Alysia didn't dare contradict him, but knew better than most that time didn't always heal. Time just made some more bitter, but she couldn't say that to Christos, and she couldn't criticize his mother, either. Mothers, especially Greek mothers, were above reproach.

Aware that he felt awkward, she sought to alleviate some of the tension. "Would you like coffee?"

"Yes, but let me make it. You're the guest."

The guest. Not his wife, but the guest.

In the kitchen she watched as he ground the beans and filled the machine's filter. He glanced at her as he turned the machine on, his expression brooding. "Alysia, it would be best if you do not discuss your father here, or in front of my parents."

"I don't understand. Is there something I should know?"

"Yes. No. It doesn't matter. Just do as I say."

Alysia could hear his mother's scathing tone echo in her head. *A good girl, not a Lemos.* She shivered. "This is personal," she said numbly. "What happened? What did my father do?"

Christos shrugged, obviously uncomfortable. "It's a long time ago."

"Not so long ago if your mother can't look at me without cursing."

"It wasn't that bad."

"Close enough." She lifted her chin, horrified to discover she was on the brink of tears. She was suddenly scared. She'd begun to feel things for Christos that she'd never felt for any man, not even Jeremy. Christos had broken through that chink in her armor. Pulled the stone from around her heart. If his family hated her they were in serious trouble. "I have a right to know. As your wife, Christos."

"Your father made it impossible for my father to get employment on Oinoussai, resulting in my father being blacklisted. He couldn't get work on the island, not ever again."

A lump lodged in her throat. "How? Why?"

"Your father was engaged in unethical business practices—"

She closed her eyes, not needing to hear another word. So Christos did know. Her father, desperate to get ahead, hired men to damage other ship owners' vessels, sabotaging sailings. When the ships couldn't sail, her father rushed in and gathered the business. "Constantine told you?"

"No. I knew long before I ever went into business with Constantine. My father was one of the welders hired to dismantle Constantine Pappas's ships."

"He should have gone to the police," she whispered, sickened at the horrible things her father had done in the name of business.

"He wouldn't, out of respect to your mother."

She felt a cold knot form inside her. "Actually I think my mother would have thanked him."

"Don't worry. Constantine and I settled our debts with your father. That's why he and I went into business together. We both needed each other. And with his help, I've had my revenge." He leaned against the counter, and smiled, but there was no warmth in his eyes, no tenderness in the twist of his lips. "I have you."

And her father's fortune.

She closed her eyes, swaying. She felt like a fool. Here she was, falling in love with Christos, while he was exacting his revenge. What an idiot she was! She never had been able to separate her body and her heart.

"Your father desperately wants grandchildren," he added tightly. "And he'll get them, but they'll be Pateras, not Lemos. Never Lemos."

Freezing inwardly she wrapped her arms around herself. "What children?" she taunted. "And from where?"

"I know you've said you can't have children but you've never been to specialists. Doctors can perform miracles these days. There are procedures—"

"Stop telling me about doctors and procedures, and listen to me!"

"I'm listening but you're not saying anything."

"Yes, I am, but you just don't want to hear it.

You want me to be like your mother, you want me to stay home and take care of things here.''

"Yes. Exactly."

"But that's what you want, not what I want. You can't dictate my life, Christos. I've a mind. I want to use it.''

"Use it by creating a home for us, a family for us—''

The back door opened, silencing him, drawing them both up short. A cheery voice shouted out a bright hello. Christos drew in a ragged breath, his hard features brittle with anger. "Mrs. Avery," he announced, his voice clipped.

They stared at each other, visibly shaken. Christos drank from his coffee cup and Alysia smoothed a hand across her skirt, trying to steady her nerves.

He married her for her body. For her ability to bear him children.

Children she wouldn't have. Seven years ago, maybe. Now? Never.

The housekeeper's low-heeled shoes clicked briskly on the hardwood floor as she entered the kitchen. Her small, plump hands busily tied her apron over her bright red dress. "Breakfast?" she asked, before catching sight of Alysia.

"Yes, please," Christos answered grimly.

The woman's round face suddenly wreathed in smiles. "The new Mrs. Pateras?"

Christos shot Alysia a dark glance. "Yes, indeed, Mrs. Avery. And now that you're here, I'll leave the new Mrs. Pateras in your capable hands.''

Alysia heard the front door slam in the middle of Mrs. Avery's house tour. Alysia stiffened, turned toward the sound.

"Don't worry. It's just Mr. Pateras leaving for work." And with a bright smile Mrs. Avery continued showing Alysia around.

The original house was over two hundred years old and had been greatly expanded and remodeled at the turn of the last century. The rooms were all large and well proportioned, the ceilings eleven and a half feet high with enormous paned windows providing spectacular views and welcoming light.

But it was hard to feel the sun's warmth when she felt so cold inside. Hard to enjoy the comfortable luxury when she couldn't forget her last conversation with Christos.

What he wanted, she realized wearily, was a traditional wife. A wife like his mother. A wife to carry his children.

Just like she'd failed her father, she'd fail Christos. The things he wanted she couldn't give.

Christos called and left a message with Mrs. Avery, telling her he wouldn't be home until seven-thirty. Mrs. Avery usually left at six, but tonight she offered to stay and serve the dinner she'd already prepared. Alysia assured the kindly housekeeper that she could dish and serve just fine and sent Mrs. Avery home.

Alone, Alysia slowly set the table, using the good china and crystal, carefully folding the linen napkins. All afternoon she'd replayed the scene in the kitchen through her head, reliving Christos's revelation that his family had suffered at the hands of her father, reliving his own revelation that he'd married her not simply for her fortune, but to exact a price on the Lemos family, to take the Lemos name and make it his.

She'd paid the ultimate price for being her father's daughter.

Numbly Alysia lit the tall tapered candles on the table, shaking her hand to extinguish the match, even as Christos appeared in the dining-room doorway.

She turned, caught a glimpse of the fatigue etched in deep lines at his mouth and eyes. His gaze took in the fresh rose centerpiece and elegant place settings. "Mrs. Avery must think we're enjoying the honeymoon."

She heard the cynicism in his voice but refused to be baited. "Would you like a glass of wine? I've opened a bottle. Mrs. Avery said you enjoy wine with your dinner."

Reluctantly he nodded. "All right, then."

She poured him a glass, handed it to him. He avoided touching her fingers.

Christos wandered around the dining-room table, sipping his wine, studying her arrangement of flowers, the linen cloth, the gleam of crystal in the flickering candlelight. "We're not celebrating anything, are we?"

"No." She felt herself begin to flush, self-conscious and embarrassed. She'd tried to please him. "You don't like the table?"

"Seems like a lot of trouble."

"It was no trouble. Growing up we always set a formal table for dinner. Nice linens. Candles."

"Ah, yes, the lives of the rich and famous."

His sarcasm stung, sending blood surging to her face. "I can't change who I am."

"Just as I can't change who I am." He sipped from his goblet.

"It was not easy being Darius Lemos's only child."

"No, of course not. It must have been awful being rich."

"Spoiled rotten, I was." She smiled at him, her jaws aching with the effort. "Dining every night with crystal and candlelight."

"We couldn't afford crystal. Candles were frivolous."

She felt wound so tightly, her body so tense she was trembling inwardly. Jerkily she leaned forward, blowing out the candles she'd just lit. The blackened wicks smoked. "Better?"

"You didn't have to do that."

"I didn't have to do that, but it's what you wanted. You're going to punish me now, every chance you can get. You're going to use every opportunity to impress upon me how desperate you were growing up and how revoltingly rich we were. You, working so hard, making something out of yourself, and me, just a spoiled little rich girl in need of a hospital and doctors to fix my self-esteem."

"Is that why you were there? Low self-esteem?"

She laughed, even as her chest tightened with hurt and pain. "Wouldn't you like to know!"

"I would, yes."

"So you can figure out why my father couldn't marry me off to a real Greek?" She caught sight of his expression, his jaw jutted, eyes narrowed in anger.

She rushed on, fueled by his coldness and her acute loneliness. "You think you have the upperhand here, but I have news for you. You were bought, Christos, you were bought because you could be bought. A self-respecting Greek wouldn't have me. A self-respecting Greek would sooner put his eye out than look upon me. But you, hungry for ships and money and power, made a deal with my father, and now you're curious, dying to know why Daddy Darius couldn't get rid of me."

"I do have some questions."

"I bet." She trembled with rage. "You, Christos Pateras, like my father, love to play God."

He said nothing, his back rigid, his dark eyes narrowed, thick lashes lowered.

"But I'm tired of you and my father making choices for me, deciding who I am, what I'll do, how I should think. I've had twenty-five years of men making decisions for me and I will not put up with it anymore."

"You're making me out to be a monster."

"Aren't you? My father was a monster. He couldn't love, or forgive. Tell me, how are you different from him?"

He said nothing, his jaw popping, his body so tense she feared he might reach for her, punish her insolence with a quick backhand the way her father used to do. But he didn't move. Didn't lift a finger.

Suddenly her anger deflated, and she felt wretched. She didn't understand why she had to lash out at him and what she'd hoped to accomplish.

This wasn't the way to his heart, that much she knew.

But she'd never have his heart. Just as she'd never have his respect.

Fighting tears, she fled to her room.

Unable to calm herself, Alysia tackled her stacks of luggage, finishing the unpacking job Mrs. Avery had begun. She was still filling the drawers in her dresser when Christos opened the bedroom door.

She'd felt him in the doorway, felt him watching her, but he didn't speak and she didn't turn around.

Her eyes burned and she blinked hard, concentrating on her task.

She'd said terrible things to him, called him terrible names, and he didn't deserve it, not all of it, at least. She was angry with him because she wanted more from him but fighting wouldn't bring him closer. It would only push him farther away.

"I've dished up dinner," he said quietly.

A lump filled her throat. "I'm really not all that hungry."

"You need to eat. Come," he repeated, extending a hand. "Let's not waste Mrs. Avery's meal."

She didn't have the strength to fight him, nor the

energy to resist. She was hungry, and tired, jetlag catching up with her, and she followed, if only to avoid further conflict.

In the dining room the candles glowed on the table, the lightbulbs in the grand crystal-and-silver chandelier dimmed. The room shone pale yellow in the flickering light and the plates on the table were filled with Mrs. Avery's roasted chicken and buttery new potatoes.

They ate in silence, each contemplative, studiously avoiding conversation.

Finally Christos pushed his plate aside. "Fifteen years ago I made a choice," he said quietly, not looking at her, but at a fixed point on the table. "It was a difficult choice."

She looked across the gleaming table, her gaze fixing on his mouth, unable to meet his eyes. He undid her. He made her want things she thought she'd given up long ago.

"I had to choose between school and sports. I'd got into Yale on an athletic scholarship."

"Baseball," she murmured.

He nodded. "I loved the game, loved being outside, on the grass, and the camaraderie of being part of a team. But I wasn't a great player. I was good, and I might have made it to the pros, but I couldn't take the risk."

He lifted his wineglass, took a sip and set the goblet down again. "If I stuck with baseball there was a good chance I'd struggle for years. I wouldn't be able to take care of my parents, and I knew without my help, my mother would spend her life scrubbing other people's toilets. I couldn't bear it. My pride couldn't bear it. My family had been through so much. I wanted more for them, more for all of us.''

"So you pursued business instead.''

"I pursued your father,'' he corrected softly, self-mockingly. "Every decision I made, every contract I signed, every investment had one purpose—to get me closer to the day I'd crush your father.''

"You hated him that much?''

"I hated what he did to my father. As you can see, I'm not a very forgiving man.''

"You don't strike me as ruthless.''

"I wasn't always.''

Had there been a different Christos then, a younger Christos who wanted less, and perhaps loved more? "I might have liked you then.''

His dark head lifted and he gazed at her from beneath a furrowed brow. His cheekbones jutted, his jaw at an angle, and even though he stared at her, she was sure he was looking inward, seeing not her, but himself, and his expression haunted her. "Maybe,'' he answered in a deep, strangled voice. "Maybe.''

She rose from her chair, wanting to go to him, but halfway around the table realized he wouldn't want her, didn't need her, not that way.

Torn, she gathered the dishes, stacking the bread plate on the dinner plate and pushing the cutlery to the middle.

"There is one other thing.'' His deep voice stilled

her jerky motions. "I wouldn't mention it except I know my mother, and I know she will."

She glanced at him over her shoulder, waiting for whatever would come next. He smiled, but the smile didn't warm his eyes. "I was engaged earlier this year, before I married you."

Dishes cradled to her tummy, she struggled to make sense of what he was saying. "Engaged to whom?"

"A local girl."

"Someone from a family like yours."

His dark head inclined. "Our mothers arranged it."

With a flash she intuited what he was really saying. "Your mother was the matchmaker."

His gaze held hers. "Yes, and our families were thrilled. They made quite a big fuss."

"I can imagine." And she could. Christos Pateras, an American-Greek tycoon, a dazzling American success story, marries local American-Greek girl. It would have been a perfect match. Even the gods would have been smiling.

"You loved her?" she whispered, hating how her body responded with pain. Why did she care? Why did she have to feel so much?

"I loved her sweetness. I loved her gentleness."

"She wanted children."

"She dreamed of a big family."

Jealousy consumed her. Alysia didn't even know this other woman and she felt wild with envy. To be the woman Christos would cherish...

But she couldn't leave it at that. She had to know more. "Was there an accident?"

"No." Christos's black brows knitted, his expression grim. "I broke it off a couple of months ago, realizing she wasn't the one for me."

Sweet relief flooded her limbs. "What changed your mind?"

"Your father."

Alysia didn't know if she dropped the dishes or if they simply fell. Either way, they came crashing down, plates rolling, cutlery clattering, one fork bouncing. Nothing, she dimly realized, broke. How fortunate.

She struggled to gather the dishes but her fingers wouldn't cooperate.

All she could see was her father, pen in hand, scribbling staggering figures on paper, promising Christos ships, wealth, more power.

She sucked in air, scalding tears filling her eyes and grabbed blindly at the fallen silverware, unable to see, unable to think.

Her father cutting a check and Christos taking it all. The deal, the marriage, the business. Not for love. But for money. For revenge.

Christos's chair scraped back. He took her arm and she jumped back, his touch setting her skin on fire.

If only she'd been the poor girl from a poor emigrant family, engaged to Christos. To be chosen for one's goodness, to be chosen for one's rightness, to be chosen and loved!

"Don't," Christos said roughly, taking her arm again.

She opened her eyes, looked at him, unaware of the tears filling her eyes. Emotion darkened his own beautiful features. "Don't what?" she whispered.

"Don't say it. Don't want it. What we have is what I wanted."

"Is it?"

"Yes."

"But what we have is nothing."

"That's not true. It's no better, no worse than any other arranged marriage."

"I can't live like this."

"Sorry. You don't have a choice."

"Don't I?"

"No. Not anymore. Not as my wife."

CHAPTER NINE

BEFORE he'd taken a step, she knew he was going to touch her, to take her into his arms and create havoc within her again. She wanted his touch as much as she dreaded it, fearing the loss of control, especially to him.

Alysia tried to escape but Christos was too quick, catching her by her arms and drawing her against his chest. His hands cupped her bottom, pulling her firmly against his hips. ''All your life you've been the poor neglected Alysia. No one to love you. No one to want you.''

He pressed her even closer to his hips, making her vividly aware of his arousal. ''But I want you, I want you more than I've ever wanted anyone.''

''You want me to punish my father—''

''I couldn't care less about your father. I want you.'' He kissed the side of her throat, his breath warm, his lips making her skin tingle.

His lips felt incredible, his mouth sending torments of feeling racing up and down her spine. He was turning her into something hot and dangerous. Her body felt electric, her nerves overly sensitized.

Helplessly she slid a hand across his chest, dazed by the warmth he created within her, and her desire to feel him, be a part of him, capture the passion she'd felt in his arms before.

"Careful," he mocked her, his voice deepening, "I might actually think you want me."

The warmth of his breath against her cheek, the mockery in his voice, the heat of his body against hers made her crave more.

As Christos's dark head dipped, she reached up, clasping his nape, a soft moan escaping her lips. She slid her fingers through his crisp, damp hair and inhaled his clean male scent.

His mouth parted hers, his tongue teasing the softness of her inner lip until her lips opened wider. She felt the core of her melt. Shameless in her desire, she shifted, rising slightly, encouraging him.

He pressed her backward, against the dining-room table, his kiss deepening, drawing her tongue into his mouth. He sucked on the tip of her tongue, creating a tight friction that echoed the throbbing in her belly and the ache between her thighs.

He sucked harder on her tongue before finding the inside of her lip. He bit the softness of her lip and she gasped, arching into him for relief.

"I do want you. I want you to make love to me," she begged, her voice thick, husky with passion.

It was all the encouragement he needed. Christos swept her into his arms and carried her up the stairs, pushing open the bedroom door, through the darkened room to his bed.

He found the warm, smooth flesh of her abdomen, unbuttoning her blouse with quick, sure fingers. His palms caressed the length of her torso, tracing the edge of her lace bra beneath the weight of each breast. Her nipples tightened, peaking with feeling, yet he grazed the nipples, bypassing them to kiss the hollow beneath. She squirmed, reaching for him, struggling to unbutton his shirt.

He helped her with his shirt, peeling the fabric from his shoulders to reveal the taut planes of his chest. Her palms slid down his hard abdomen to his belt buckle and with shaking hands she unfastened the buckle and then his trousers.

He sucked in his breath when she found him, her hand wrapping around his hard satin length. He drew her hand away, whispering, ''Not yet,'' and lowered his own head to savor the sensitive hollow between her breasts, his tongue drawing circles of fire, around and around until she clamped her knees together in futile desire.

He finished off her blouse, pushing the silk fabric aside, and then unhooked the lace bra, sending that to the floor as well. The air felt cool against her heated skin and she reached for him, drawing him back down to her.

When his mouth covered one tight bud, she responded blindly, helplessly dragging her nails down his torso, lightly raking the carved plane of his chest, and small hard nipples.

She was slick with need by the time he knelt between her thighs. ''No more anything,'' she whispered, ''I just want you.''

He entered her slowly, trying to give her time to

adjust to his body, but she didn't need much time, welcoming the exquisite sensation of fullness.

Her body felt lovely and alive, her muscles suffused with warmth, her skin incredibly sensitive. Every place he touched her glowed. Every kiss made her crave more.

"Am I hurting you?" he demanded hoarsely.

"No," she answered, pressing a finger to his lovely lips, stilling his speech. "Just love me."

And he did, bracing himself on his hands, thrusting deeply inside, first slowly and then faster, creating alternating torments of fullness and need, drawing them together, building the tension, building the reward.

His mouth returned to hers, and she answered his kiss with near desperation, lifting her hips to meet him, relishing the tenderness and passion.

She knew then she'd always love him, heart and soul, or the part of her soul not destroyed with Alexi.

"Christos," she whispered urgently, drawing him deeper inside her, opening her mouth, giving him all of her body since he wouldn't take her heart.

The vivid swirling sensations built to a feverish pitch, his thrusts harder, faster, and for long mindless seconds she was at an insurmountable peak, nearing climax, her body warm, damp, straining against his, but not yet set free.

Christos plunged into her yet again, moving deeply, and suddenly she was his, all his, exploding in brilliant, breathtaking pleasure. Her pleasure sent him over the edge, and they came together, their bodies shuddering with rippling sensation, satiated and exhausted.

Still tangled together, her heart racing wildly, Christos kissed her again, long and hard. "Mine," he whispered against her mouth. "Remember that." And then his tongue rasped against hers in one final mind-spinning kiss that drew shivers down her spine, warmth from her belly, and flexed her toes.

He settled her to one side of him, pulling her hip in against his, one palm cupping her breast. For a long moment neither moved, nor spoke, their warm, weary bodies relaxed.

Alysia felt herself spiral down, down, down, but she never crashed, just floated in lovely suspended sensation, aware of Christos's fingers trailing in the curve of her lower back, and gently caressing the swell of her hip.

"You are worth all the ships in the world," he murmured, his voice husky, and she turned her head to look up at him, surprised by his words, but before she could ask him what he meant, he was breathing deeply, black lashes fanning his cheekbones. He was asleep.

They made love again later, toward the end of the night. Neither spoke, their bodies communicating in wordless expression. But later, after they'd recovered from the intensity of the physical pleasure, Christos pressed a kiss to the top of her head and eased out of bed.

"Where are you going?" she asked, sleepily sitting forward, sheet drawn to her breasts.

"Work."

"Now? It's so early!"

"It's five. I've a lot to do. Better to get started."

She sat up higher, pushed a fistful of hair out of her eyes. "Can I come?"

"No. Go back to sleep. You need the rest."

She pushed back the bedcovers, pressed her hands to her knees. "I could help you. You could put me to work."

"You know nothing about the industry."

"So teach me." She was warming to the idea, realizing she could try to win him over. Christos was like her father. He equated business with success, and he respected successful people. If she could find a way to be useful, contribute to his business, he might see her as more than Darius Lemos's spoiled daughter.

He might realize she had a brain. He might respect her.

He might even fall in love with her.

"Please, Christos, give me a chance."

"This is not a good day for show and tell. Today I have important conferences scheduled. Union bosses waiting to rip my head off. It's a day of hard bargaining, a little bloodletting—hopefully not my own. You'd be in the way. You'd be a distraction."

His good mood quickly evaporated as his wife flung herself from bed, her slim figure lunging at the floor, grabbing for her clothes. "I wouldn't be a distraction. I wouldn't get in your way. Christos, please."

"Alysia, be serious."

Her hands shook as she picked up her panties and stepped into the tiny scraps of satin. "I am. Completely serious."

"Alysia, you're a woman."

Daggers flashed in her dark blue eyes and with a furious glance in his direction, she yanked her white silk blouse over her shoulders, forgetting her strappy lace bra, the fabric hugging her breasts, outlining the full, round shape. "I can't believe you just said that!"

"I watched my mother slave on her knees in other people's bathrooms. She worked her fingers to the bone and I vowed that when I married, my wife would never work, never be humiliated like that."

"I want to go into the office, not clean bathrooms." Her full, swollen nipples pressed tautly against the thin silk fabric and he felt his body harden, responding to her beauty and passion, unfazed by her anger.

"No. I will provide for us because I *can* provide for us. That is how it should be, and that is how it will be. Understood?"

With a strangled oath she flung her navy skirt at him. He caught it easily.

"Then go!" she spat, tossing her head, long silky hair swinging over her shoulders. "Do whatever it is you must do, but don't expect to come home and find me waiting!"

He stopped where he was, two steps from the foot

of the bed, desire dying. He hadn't heard right. She was threatening him again. Unbelievable.

One of his hands circled her slim upper arm and he dragged her toward him. Her bare legs kicked, her hands pounded on his chest. "What did you say?"

"You heard me."

Anger swept through him, anger and impatience. He tilted her head back, holding her face captive beneath his. His kiss was an assault as much as it was an insult. He kissed her hard, a savagery in the rake of his tongue and grind of his lips. He wanted her to feel his wrath, wanted to remind her that in this house, he was the man, and she, the woman.

But even as he probed her mouth, his hard embrace gentled, his fingers releasing her chin to cup her cheek. She felt unbelievable in his arms, tasted like honey and crushed almonds. She was sweet and damn it, she was his.

She'd been his ever since she'd interrupted her father's meeting all those years ago. He knew then he wanted her, wanted her to be his. He'd protect her. He'd cherish her. He'd keep Darius Lemos from hurting her again.

Alysia's swollen mouth trembled beneath his, her slim body quivering against his bare chest. His kiss softened and he caressed the length of her neck, stroking her satiny skin, her body shuddering at each slow, lingering touch, playing her tenderly the way one would play the violin. She was melting in his arms, melting into him, and gently he released her.

He exhaled slowly, his breathing ragged, his heart

pounding with the same fierceness that it surged through his limbs, gathering in his groin. God, he wanted her, wanted to take her and taste her, make love to her until she surrendered completely, admitting that she wanted no one but him, no life but theirs.

But she wouldn't meet him, not even halfway, and as much as he wanted to kiss her senseless, there wasn't time.

His brows flattened as he pressed the tip of his finger to her quivering mouth. "Do not, my rebellious wife, threaten to leave me again."

She heard the hardness in his tone and realized she'd pushed him too far. Shivering, she drew her blouse even tighter across her chest, wanting him yet again, craving him still. She should have more pride, want more from him than just sex, but desperate woman that she was, she took whatever he gave her, even the crumbs from his table.

Disgusted with herself, she lashed out. "I gave you what you wanted. You wanted me to perform my wifely duties, well, I did. I serviced you. Now give me what I want."

Christos stared at her, stunned, his expression revealing hurt, and betrayal. Then his dark eyes shuttered, leaving his chiseled features starkly remote. But she'd seen enough in his eyes to know her barb hit home. She'd wounded him.

Instead of joy, she felt remorse, and fresh shame. Before she could apologize, he was walking away, putting distance between them.

He headed for his bathroom, flicked on the lights and heat lamp before turning on the shower. She followed him into the bathroom, unsettled by what had just taken place between them.

The cold tile floor curled her toes. "Christos—"

Steam rose from the open shower door, fogging the white tiled bath. Christos turned to look at her. He was naked but completely uninhibited. "We have an expression in America. It's called 'low blow.' It means, you've hit below the belt. Do you understand what I'm saying?"

She swallowed hard, wondering how something so lovely, what took place in his bed, could now turn into something so ugly. "Yes, but—"

"Hitting below the belt is not acceptable. Not in this marriage. Not ever."

"I'm sorry, but you—"

"Like a child. So defiant. So unwilling to bend."

"Is that how you accept an apology?"

"Is that how you give an apology?"

She couldn't stand it, couldn't stand the way he made her feel so inadequate. "I hate you," she whispered, tears starting to her eyes. "I hate you and everything you stand for."

"Trust me. At the moment, the feeling's mutual." His dark lashes lowered, concealing his expression. "It didn't have to be like this, Alysia."

Tears shimmered in her eyes as she flung her head back. "Is that an apology?"

"No. A statement of fact."

"Why didn't you marry your good American-Greek girl and leave me in the convent?"

His mouth flattened, his dark eyes narrowing as his gaze raked her half-naked body. "I couldn't."

"You and my father are exactly alike. You love money before all else!"

"I tried to love you. But you won't let anybody near you. You won't allow someone to be kind—"

"Is that what you were showing me in bed? Kindness?" She laughed, her voice high and strained, a hint of hysteria in the thin pitch. "Well, from now on, I can do without your acts of kindness." She balled her hands into fists. "Call a spade, a spade. Our marriage is nothing but a business deal. Dollars. Numbers. A bank account. What happened in there, in that bed, was nothing more than a business transaction."

His cheekbones jutted against the pallor of his skin. His nostrils flared with each short, ragged breath. "Fine, it's business. But it's an ongoing business. I'll take you when I want, and how I want, and to hell with the kindness you despise."

He pulled her into the shower with him, holding her beneath the blast of jets, water soaking them both, drenching her blouse, outlining her breasts.

Turning, he shifted her body behind his to take the brunt of the water. Clasping her face in his hands, he covered her mouth with his, lips parting her, tongue stabbing at her mouth's softness, taking her without pretense of tenderness.

The water beat down around them, splashing their bodies, dripping down their legs.

When Christos finally lifted his head, he slowly pressed a kiss to the corner of her throbbing mouth. His black eyelashes were spiky wet, his jaw glistening with water. "From now on I'll expect you to be ready for me, just like my banker's always on call, ready for my business."

"You're an ass," she whispered, hurt, and yet hungry for more skin, more pressure, more of him.

"And you're my wife." He unbuttoned her soggy blouse, dropping it in a puddle at their feet.

She tried to climb out of the shower. He pulled her back in, blocking the door with his body. He picked up a bar of soap and began lathering it between his large hands. He worked the soap into thick white suds, and then held the bar above her body. The foaming suds spilled from his hands to her shoulders and dripped down her breasts.

His gaze lowered, his burning gaze following the path of the bubbles as they slid down the sweep of breasts, her taut aching nipples peeking through soapy foam.

Reaching out to her, Christos traced the bubble path, his firm sudsy palm against her breast and distended nipple. He drew his hands across her, spreading the soapy lather down her flat abdomen, into the soft mound at the apex of her thighs. He washed her clean, rinsed the soap off, and lifted her chin. "I've washed you, I've made you mine. Your life, Alysia, is with me."

Shivering, she left the shower and wrapped a towel around herself and squeezed the extra water from her hair. Christos stepped past her, his hips bumping her bottom and she quickly moved out of the way. Reaching across her, he pulled a towel off the bar. "You have a half hour," he said flatly, no expression in his voice.

"A half hour?"

He looked at her with anger, and scorn. "Until we go. I won't leave you here and give you a second chance to run away. So you win, Alysia. You're going to work with me even though I don't like it one little bit."

CHAPTER TEN

DURING the helicopter ride into the city, Christos avoided looking at her, and she kept her chin firmly lifted, refusing to let him see that her hard-earned victory tasted terribly bitter.

She'd wanted to be a part of his world, but not at this price. Never at this price.

The moment they arrived at his office, walking through the frosted glass doors into a modern office furnished in navy, burgundy and cream, they joined a meeting already in progress and remained in the conference room all day.

Christos didn't glance her way during the three-hour-long discussion with the shipworker's union boss. And the discussion, so heated that at times she feared the union boss would come to blows, made her incredibly uneasy. But Christos remained utterly calm. He addressed the others without rancor, and yet he didn't bend, nor did he compromise.

The meeting adjourned for ten minutes so all could move around the room, use the bathroom, stretch their legs. Christos stood up, walked to the phone on the corner table, a table just inches from her chair, and made a series of brief phone calls without once looking at her.

Concluding his calls, he returned to his chair, again without a glance in her direction.

It was as if he was telling her, without so many words, that she could push him all she wanted, but that would never change the way he felt about her. He despised her. Clearly she meant nothing to him.

A bitter pill for a bitter victory.

They were silent on the ride home in the helicopter, landing on the cement pad in Christos's estate only twenty minutes after having taken off from the Manhattan skyscraper.

A car waited for them at the landing pad, driving them the short distance to the house. Mrs. Avery opened the door, welcomed them cheerfully, offering an appetizer tray and cold drinks.

Christos took his glass, and Alysia's, thanking Mrs. Avery with a warmth that Alysia couldn't miss.

"Mr. Pateras, your mother called late this afternoon to let you know your father had to work late tonight. She didn't think they'd be here much before eight."

"Thank you, Mrs. Avery. I know you've had a long day. Please don't feel you need to stay."

"But I can, and then you and Mrs. Pateras could relax a little. Unwind before your parents arrive."

Christos shot Alysia a speculative look. "We'll relax, don't you worry about us."

The moment Mrs. Avery was gone Christos ordered Alysia upstairs.

Her eyebrows shot up. Her stomach a bundle of nerves. "Pardon me?"

"Can you walk, or shall I carry you again?"

"You want me to go upstairs now, just before your parents come?"

He smiled coldly, no warmth in his dark eyes. "We've a good solid hour."

"You've got to be joking."

"Sweetheart, I never joke about sex."

I never joke about sex. How much cruder could one be? Her eyes smarted. Her throat closed, bottling the air in her lungs. "I'm sorry, but I'm not exactly in the mood."

He tossed back his drink, and shrugged. "Then get in the mood, because we made a deal. Business, right, sweetheart? You wanted to be a part of my world, well, I'm going to be a part of yours. I want you. Now."

"Don't do this."

"Why not? You treat me with as much contempt." He made a rough sound in his throat, reaching forward to run his finger across her cheek. "Ah, there it is, the anger. The hatred. It's all there, just for me." Christos turned, began climbing the stairs. "Now come. Business is business."

She wanted to hate him, wanted to shout something at him, but her voice failed her and her heart ached, craving something else from him than this.

As he took the stairs, she watched the length of his back, the powerful legs, and despite the anger and anguish burning within her, she felt another emotion, one awakened by the caress on her cheek.

She wanted him. She wanted to feel him over her,

against her, the warm, hard planes of his body, her own warm acceptance. And slowly she followed him up the stairs.

They made love the first time with savage intent, nails raking, teeth nipping, kisses fierce and bruising. But after the first shattering orgasm, after the anger abated, Christos turned to her again, his touch softer, his expression almost gentle. He made love to her once more, this time giving rather than taking, kissing her through her second climax, holding her while she shuddered against him, murmuring assurances in her ear.

She nearly fell asleep in his arms but Christos stirred, and drawing back the covers reminded her that his parents would arrive in the next half hour.

He'd left the room and she bathed, but instead of dressing, she'd returned to the bed, curled on the foot in her towel.

She wanted more from Christos than skin. More than his mouth and fingers, his incredible satin and steel body. She wanted his heart, too.

But this marriage, their marriage, was paper and money, ships and inheritance. It wasn't love, would never be love. It was just business. Business and vengeance.

Her eyes burned, her throat sealed closed, and digging her nails into her palms she felt like the poor little rich girl again, the young Greek heiress whose fortune couldn't even protect her infant son.

God, how she hated her inheritance, hated the pampered world of nothingness.

The door to her room opened. Christos stood in the doorway, buttoning the sleeves of his crisp white shirt, the tail of it already tucked into dark wool trousers. "Alysia, you can't afford to dawdle. My parents will be here very soon. And trust me, you won't endear yourself to my mother if she finds you undressed."

She couldn't move, couldn't tear her gaze from him. He looked so cool and calm, so perfectly controlled, while she felt like a ball of warm wax, soft and changing, helpless in his hands.

She still felt him everywhere in her, on her, near her. She felt his mouth and hands, felt her body respond, and the dull pain in her heart.

Covering her heartache, she gave him a defiant glare. "Why not? You undressed me."

"Fine. I'll dress you. So much for independence, Mrs. Pateras." He stalked to her closet, plucking a silk skirt and cropped jacket from hangers.

"Wear these," he said, tossing them at her before digging through her drawers for appropriate lingerie. "My father loves lavender and my mother dislikes trousers. Wear your hair down but not too much makeup. I expect to see you downstairs in fifteen minutes tops. Am I clear?"

"Christos—"

"Am I clear?"

"Yes." She swallowed, gathering courage. "Your father, he must hate me very much."

He stopped at the door, but didn't turn around. "My father has no vendetta against you. My father is a compassionate man. A man far more tolerant than I.''

He glanced back at her, his hard, handsome features without expression, his dark eyes intent, focused on her, observing the sudden tension at her mouth. ''My father will be kind to you. Do not worry about him.''

''And your mother?''

''She answers to my father.''

Like a good woman should.

He didn't say the last part, but it hung there, unspoken between them. She smiled painfully. ''I'll try not to embarrass you tonight.''

''Just don't run away.''

Downstairs she found Christos uncorking a bottle of red wine. Headlights gleamed in the driveway, reflecting through the dining-room window.

''They're here,'' he announced unnecessarily.

She stiffened, frightened at coming face-to-face with people her father had hurt so deeply. ''Tell me what to say to your mother. Tell me how to act.''

''Just be yourself,'' he said quietly. Her head jerked up. Her eyes met his. ''My mother will be happy when I'm happy,'' he added more gently.

But I won't ever make you happy, she silently answered him, her heart aching, emotions so raw and new that she struggled to keep them in check. ''Christos, it's not all business, is it?''

''You mean between us?''

Silence stretched, a humiliation of its own. Car doors slammed outside. Footsteps on the brick steps.

Bands of color burned her cheekbones. "Yes. Between us."

More silence. The shockingly loud ring of the doorbell. The knowledge that his parents were there, waiting, just on the other side of the door.

He didn't even glance at the door. "No. It's not just business."

She felt a bubble of emotion rise, higher, fuller, hope and pain, tenderness, too.

He crossed to the door but didn't open it, his gaze still on her, as if able to read her chaotic emotions. "I didn't marry Maria just because your father offered me money, and I didn't marry you to punish your family. I married you because I wanted you." And then, just like that, he swung the front door open, inviting his parents in.

Dinner with his parents was less of a disaster than she'd expected. With his father present, Christos's mother was subdued, silently following the conversation while Christos's father discussed business and matters of the church with Christos.

The elder Mr. Pateras made efforts to include Alysia, listening thoughtfully to her point of view, and treating her with what seemed to be genuine warmth and respect.

Following dinner they shared a sweet liqueur, a drink Christos said was made locally by a Greek family. Then his parents left after Christos and Alysia saw them to the door.

They stood together in the entry, neither moving from the door. After a long moment Christos leaned forward to tuck a tendril of golden hair behind her ear. "That wasn't so bad," he said

"No. Your father is lovely."

"I don't know if lovely is the right word, but it's obvious he likes you. I'm glad. I'd hoped he would."

"But your mother..."

"My mother is notoriously hard to please. With babies, grandchildren, I promise you, she'll have a change of heart."

Her own heart twisted, feeling like a traitor. She should talk to Christos, really talk to him, but how? What would she say? How could she tell him the truth? In some ways he was modern, open-minded, strong. But in other ways, when it came to women and family, he was impossibly protective. Almost chauvinistic. If she confessed to him, she knew she'd lose him.

Christos lifted her face in his hands, his expression somber. Then his head dipped and he kissed her with heart-shattering tenderness, savoring her lips, promising a warmth and a tangible hunger.

She clung to him, needing him, and as she kissed him, tears slid from beneath her closed lashes, spilling onto her cheeks.

Christos drew back, forehead furrowing. "What's wrong?"

She couldn't tell him. Words would only destroy the tentative bonds between them. Instead she drew his head down to hers again, covering his mouth with her own.

His lips felt damp and tasted salty from her tears,

and a primitive emotion compelled her to kiss him deeply, sampling the trace of her tears on his skin. She tasted herself, and him, and it stirred dormant emotions, deep-rooted emotions of love and longing. She wanted him, to belong to him, not just now, but always.

The intensity of their lovemaking that night affected them both, but for Alysia, it was life-changing. She knew she'd never want any man, or love any man, the way she loved Christos. He was a perfect combination of strength and passion, pride and tenderness.

They made love again and his hands, body and mouth drove her to a shattering climax. Afterward, he kissed her on the damp brow before returning to her lips.

"You might not know it, but you need me, Alysia, just as much as I need you."

She lay on the crook of her arm, gazing at him in the dark. She could see his eyes and the flash of white teeth, and she leaned forward to kiss his mouth, closing the distance between them. "I know, at least the part about me needing you."

She felt him tense, his breath catching, holding. At last he exhaled, his hand rising to her face, stroking her cheek, her skin still glowing with the heat of passion.

"I want to have a baby with you. I want to make a family with you."

Fear gripped her heart and she pressed her fingertips to his mouth to keep him from saying more.

"But you know that," he said. "You know it's what I want more than anything."

"I'm not mother-material," she answered hoarsely.

"That's not true. You're just afraid you can't conceive, but I'm sure with the right doctors, with new treatments—"

"Christos, you don't know!"

"What don't I know?"

The truth... You don't know anything.

"Alysia, you're my wife. I want you. I want a family with you."

Her eyes scalded, hot and gritty, and she tipped her forehead against his, hiding her face from him, hiding her past. If he knew the truth, he'd hate her, despise her.

"Talk to me," he whispered, drawing away and rolling her over onto her back. Lifting a strand of hair from the hollow of her neck, he pressed it to his mouth and then kissed her collarbone before kissing her mouth. "Trust me."

"I do." And she did, as much as she could trust anyone. *But what about the birth control pills?* A little voice whispered inside her head, stirring fresh panic. *He should know you're taking contraception.*

But another voice inside her protested. *He doesn't need to know now. You'll tell him someday, someday when he'll understand...*

"I'd do anything for you."

"Shh, you can't say such things."

"I can, because I love you."

She lay still, frozen, not daring to breathe. He couldn't have just said what she thought he said. It was her imagination, her need for acceptance, and forgiveness. Because he couldn't love her, not the real Alysia. The real Alysia destroyed those she loved.

"Look at me," Christos urged, his voice husky, firm fingers on her chin, turning her face to his, not understanding the tears in her eyes or the pain snaking through her heart. "We'll make a baby, and we'll be happy. I promise."

The weeks passed quickly; Christos was attentive, his desire something tangible and real. They slept together, woke together, took their meals together, and still neither could get enough of the other, seeking each other's company, wanting more touch, more passion, more pleasure.

After that stormy first week they'd managed to become friends, developing a relationship out of the artifice.

Christos invited Alysia to join him once or twice a week at his office, making a point of including her in big meetings, and other times, bringing home business reports and financial statements to discuss with her.

She found Christos's perspective on business fascinating, yet was bored by the myriad of details. While she liked understanding why he made certain decisions, she didn't want to pore over numbers or challenge his economic predictions. The fact was, his business bored her. What's worse, the endless columns of numbers looked meaningless after a while, just number after number, like little ants marching across the page.

"I hate this," she muttered, slamming the proposal closed and tossing it at the foot of the couch. "I can't stand it. There's nothing about this business that I enjoy."

Christos turned from the window where he'd been admiring the sunset, his mouth twisting. "I wondered how long it'd take for you to confess." He plucked the spiral-bound booklet from the couch and flipped through it, briefly scanning the charts and graphs. "Why don't you paint again?"

His tone was deceptively mild. She glanced at him, frowned. "You know I don't paint anymore."

"We could build a studio for you here—"

"I don't want a studio," she interrupted, jumping from the couch to confront him. "I don't paint. I'll never paint again."

"I thought you trusted me."

"I do."

"Then perhaps you can explain these," he said flatly. Something had changed in his voice, his quiet tone taking an edge. "I found these in your bathroom drawer." He drew a small plastic case from his pocket, lifted them high and tapped the plastic case with a finger. "These pills aren't iron tablets, are they?"

She went hot, then cold. "No." They were her pills. Her birth control pills. He knew, too, what her bottle of iron tablets looked like.

"Where did you get them? When did you get them?"

"In Athens." She swallowed hard. "From the doctor that visited me at your house, after I fainted."

"You've been on birth control pills for the last month?" His voice echoed hard, brittle, just like his features.

"Yes." She lifted her head, flinched when she met his gaze, fury blazing in his dark eyes.

"You lied to me."

"I didn't lie."

"You weren't honest."

No, she hadn't been honest, and it was all going to come out. She saw that now. The skeletons, the nightmare, the terror. The bones were stacked too high against the closet door and the door had been opened, just a crack, but a crack was more than enough to destroy her fragile control.

She turned, opened the door to his study and began walking away, quickly, heading for the stairs and the sanctuary of her room.

Christos followed her to the stairs, and she ran up the steps, flying as fast as she could.

He covered the stairs in half the time, able to climb three steps to her one. Grasping her by her shoulders, he spun her to face him. "What the hell is going on?"

"You don't know, and you don't want to know."

"Damn it, Alysia, I've had it with your secrets and your cryptic answers." His fingers held her fast, no escaping him now. "No more riddles. I want answers. Truthful answers. Why didn't you tell me you were on the pill?''

''Because you'd have taken them away, or tried to talk me out of them—''

''Yes!''

''That's why.''

''But you knew I wanted children.''

''And you knew I couldn't give them to you!''

She yanked away, stepping blindly backward. She teetered on the top step, losing her balance. Christos caught her, pulling her roughly after him to the relative safety of her bedroom.

''No more pills, no more protection,'' he said, shutting the door behind them. ''Do you understand?''

''I understand what you're saying, but I can't do what you're asking me to do.''

''You mean you won't?''

She saw the hurt flicker in his dark eyes before being replaced by anger. ''Please, Christos, trust me—''

''Like you've trusted me?'' He turned away, covered his face with one hand. ''God, I am a fool.'' He shook his head, dropping his hand. ''Your father warned me you'd run away. He warned me you weren't very stable. But I didn't believe him. If only I had!''

''It would have saved us both a lot of trouble,'' she answered quietly, finding her pride, and her backbone.

She'd known from the beginning their marriage

wouldn't last. She knew he'd discover the truth sooner or later and the relationship would end, as swiftly, as painfully, as it had begun. Only she hadn't expected to lose her heart to him. She'd never meant to fall so madly in love.

He stared at her as if he'd never seen her before, his dark eyes stripping her to the bone. "You were never going to have my child, were you?"

"No."

"How long would you have let me wait?"

Forever, she heard the answer whisper inside herself, forever, if it meant I could be with you. Instead she shook her head. "I don't know. Until you pushed for the truth."

"So you would have continued taking the pills, getting your period, letting me believe we couldn't conceive."

"Yes."

"God, I hate you."

She shriveled on the inside, dying. "I know."

"You can't. You have no idea how much you disgust me."

"I have a faint idea," she whispered, knowing he couldn't break what was already broken, and her heart had been shattered years ago. But still he was digging a fresh hole, dirt for her grave.

He closed the distance between them, lifted his hand as if to strike her and instead caught her face in his hands, kissing her hard on the mouth. "Why?" he demanded against her trembling lips. "Just tell me why. Let me understand."

His mouth felt so warm against hers, his skin smelling of cologne and musk and she reached up to cling to his chest, needing him more than she'd ever needed anyone.

But he didn't want her touching him, and he caught her wrists, pulling her hands off him. "I'm waiting."

"You don't want to know, oh, Christos, it's bad—"

"I don't care. I just want the truth."

She gazed at him helplessly, knowing she'd lose him—no, she'd already lost him—but fear held her back. She'd kept her secret so long, told no one, not even her father, what had happened in that Paris studio that unbelievable afternoon.

"Tell me."

Her heart lurched, her mouth so dry, it tasted of cotton. Where to begin? What to say first? "I...I had a baby."

"You what?"

The adrenaline surging through her veins threatened to make her ill. She couldn't look at Christos, didn't dare take a glimpse into his face. "Had a baby. A little boy."

"When?"

"With Jeremy. We were married, had been married for a little over a year when Alexi was born."

"And?"

"I lost him."

"Stillbirth?"

"No." She shivered, chilled, wondering how

she'd ever get the words out, not wanting to see
Alexi, not wanting the horrible pictures to fill her
head again. "I delivered him, loved him, raised him.
I took him on my jobs. He had his first birthday. And
then..."

"And then what, Alysia?" Christos ground out,
shaking her, almost violent in his impatience to hear
the rest.

"I killed him."

CHAPTER ELEVEN

CHRISTOS couldn't believe it. He demanded the story again and again, ignoring her sobs, oblivious to her anguish, insisting she explain it all once more, from the beginning.

He struggled to piece her past together. She ran away with Jeremy after meeting him in Paris. They married thinking they could make a living by painting. That part made sense. That much was clear. But the rest of it...

"Christos, please, no more—"

He saw her cowering on the bed, but felt nothing for her. "How did the baby drown?" he demanded again.

"In water, in the bath—"

"You said the sink."

"Yes, in the sink. He'd been taking a bath."

"No, he wasn't taking a bath, you were giving him a bath."

"Yes."

"And what happened?"

"He drowned."

"How?"

"You know how! His little chair broke, I think. Or he wasn't in his chair—I forget, Christos, it's been so long."

"Not that long. Five years."

She closed her eyes, hugging herself. "Let me go," she whispered. "Let me go, let me go."

"I want to hear this. I want to know how you let your baby drown."

"I can't tell you."

"You can. You will." He stalked toward her, his face dark with anger. "Did the phone ring? Someone came to the door? How did you forget him?"

"Stop it!"

"How could you do it? How could you let your baby drown?"

"I was painting!" she screamed, her voice shrieking so high that it sounded like breaking glass. "I was painting."

"You were painting?" Christos stared at her aghast.

"I killed Alexi because I had to paint."

A doctor came, and Christos's parents. Alysia lay huddled in her darkened bedroom, unwilling to eat, or turn on a light. She wanted only to be left alone.

But the voices could be heard through her closed door, murmurs and exclamations, urgency in Christos, disgust in his mother's.

Sometime later the doctor entered her room, and despite her protests, turned on the light and checked her vitals. His examination was brief but thorough, shining a miniature flashlight into her eyes, listening to her chest, and taking her pulse yet again. Finally he asked her if she'd been taking any other medications lately, other than her birth control pills.

"No," she answered dully, just wanting him to go, wanting to be alone again.

But the doctor didn't move. "I understand you were in a hospital in Switzerland. Were you on something then?"

"Only when they first checked me into the hospital. It was a sedative…I fell apart at the funeral." Her shoulders lifted, a listless shrug.

The doctor didn't speak and lifting her head, her gaze met his. She expected revulsion in his expression. Instead she found only pity. Suddenly her eyes welled with tears and she begged him to go.

"I think you should rest," he said.

"I don't want to sleep."

The doctor sat down next to her on the bed. "Everyone makes mistakes."

"A mistake is burning toast."

"Good people can make tragic mistakes."

"Not like this." The tears filling her eyes clung to her lashes, blurring her vision. Every breath she drew felt like an agony. Every beat of her heart reminded her of what she'd taken from her own child. "I loved him," she sobbed. "I loved him more than I loved myself and yet look what I did—"

In her grief she hadn't heard the door open, or notice Christos standing silently in the doorway. She didn't hear when he stepped out again, soundlessly shutting the door behind him.

"I think," the doctor said quietly, gently pushing

her back, settling her against the pillows. "You must rest now. Tomorrow talk about the future."

Alysia woke to a sunlit room, the curtains drawn back to welcome the warm light. Her head felt heavy, her brain groggy, and slowly she slid from the bed to stagger to the bathroom.

She caught a glimpse of herself in the mirror. Pale face, dark, sunken eyes, white pinched lips. She looked like a corpse. Then suddenly she saw Alexi, floating face up beneath the water, eyes open, mouth open, tiny hands outstretched and her knees buckled as she screamed, shrieking at the flood of memory.

A woman in black appeared—Mrs. Pateras, Alysia dimly registered—to take her by the arm, and firmly lead her from the bathroom back to bed.

Muttering in Greek, she pushed Alysia down and handed her a cup of tea. "Drink."

Alysia's hand trembled as she clutched the hot cup. "Christos?" she whispered, disoriented by the intensity of her emotions and the realization that she'd probably lost Christos forever.

"Gone," Mrs. Pateras answered coldly.

"Where?"

The older woman pushed Alysia's legs under the covers and drew the sheet up, and then the feather duvet. "Business."

Business. "Where?"

"Greece. Something to do with ships."

Ships, there'd always be ships. Ships, contracts, profit and loss. Tears filled Alysia's eyes. How could life be so black-and-white when she lived in shades of gray?

She missed Christos, needed to see him, talk to him. He was the one person she trusted. The one she loved most. "When is he coming back?"

"I don't know."

"I'd like the phone number of his Manhattan office."

"He's not there," Mrs. Pateras answered sharply. "I told you that already, now rest, or I shall tell Christos how difficult you've been."

The bedroom felt cold after Mrs. Pateras left, the corners swathed in shadows. How difficult she's been. Same words her father used to say. Alysia the difficult. But was she really that difficult? Was wanting love such a bad thing?

Alysia closed her eyes but she couldn't sleep, consumed by memory, confused by time. How could she have turned her back on Alexi? How could she have forgotten him?

It didn't make sense. She'd been a good mother, or at least, she'd tried to be a good mother. She never let him sit in wet diapers. She never skipped on his naps. Never left him out too long in the sun. She'd been young, but she'd really tried her best.

Until that day. That one day...

All this time later and she could still feel the weight of him, feel his limp body as she pulled him from the sink. She'd run with him into the streets screaming, *God, someone, anyone, help me. Help my baby. Help my baby.*

The day of the funeral, she destroyed her easel and canvases, shredding the paintings with a pair of sharp scissors, slicing them like a madwoman into long, tangled shreds.

As she destroyed her work, she howled, her agonized cries drawing the neighbors, and then the police. It was then they gave her the shot to calm her, and bundled her off to the hospital in Bern. They said she'd been talking gibberish, but it wasn't gibberish. She'd been weeping for Alexi, promising him she'd never forget him, and never ever paint again.

And she'd kept that vow.

Alysia woke to bathe and eat. Mrs. Pateras was there, presiding over the house, overseeing Alysia's meals, her iron tablets. She determined the routine, making it clear she was the mistress of the house, not Alysia.

Alysia didn't have the strength to argue. She was still struggling to put together pieces of the past, wondering at the gaps in her memory, even as she dreaded reliving the pain. But there were too many holes in her memory, places where nothing fit and nothing made sense.

But now that the guilt had been fully awakened, she couldn't rest. Nor find peace. It felt as though she were on fire on the inside, her own form of hell.

Lying in bed was only making it worse. She had to get busy again, needed exercise, sunlight, work to do.

On the third day after the horrible confession Alysia appeared downstairs for breakfast. Mrs. Avery beamed with pleasure but Mrs. Pateras blocked the doorway to the dining room. "The doctor said you were to rest," she said stiffly.

Alysia felt a ball of tension form in her belly. She didn't want to fight with her mother-in-law, but she wasn't going to sit around any longer feeling sorry for herself. What had happened, had happened, and awful as it was, it wouldn't bring back Alexi.

"Mrs. Pateras, I appreciate all you're doing for me, but I think it's time I began to act like a normal human being again. Hiding in my room will not bring Alexi back, and it will not help me forget."

"Some things you'll never forget."

She met Mrs. Pateras' unforgiving gaze and flinched inwardly but held her ground. "It was a mistake, a dreadful mistake, but I'm not going to give up on life. I love Christos—"

"He doesn't love you. How could he?"

It was exactly her own fear, shouted at her in contempt. Alysia wavered, glanced at the stairs, and the front door behind her, then turned her back on the escape routes. There was no escape. She had to face herself, and the future. "It's none of your business," she answered quietly, far more calmly than she felt. "This is between your son and me."

The housekeeper disappeared into the kitchen and Mrs. Pateras took a step toward her, her finger pointed in accusation. "My son deserves better than you. He deserves a real woman."

"I am a real woman. I just happened to make a terrible mistake."

"You murdered your child. That's not a mistake, that's a crime!"

"I can't change the past. But I can promise Christos loyalty, and love—"

"Do you honestly believe my son will ever be happy with you? Do you think he'll ever trust you?"

Mrs. Pateras was right, Alysia realized with a shudder, she wasn't thinking about Christos's needs, just her own. Christos deserved happiness. He was a good man, a loving man, he deserved a wife he could trust.

Sick to her stomach, Alysia turned away, headed for the stairs, hurrying back to her bedroom. At her closet she yanked clothes from hangers, a long gray skirt and a loose-fitting cashmere sweater in a paler shade.

Mrs. Pateras followed her into the bedroom. "If you were smart, you'd go now, before he returns. He could get an annulment, have a proper marriage."

"Leave," Alysia choked, facing her closet, her voice failing her. "I do not want you in here, nor do I need you here. Please leave now."

"Yes, Mother, please leave now." Christos appeared in the doorway, a dark coat over his arm, a briefcase in one hand. He looked exhausted, and pained. "I heard you, Mother, all the way into the kitchen. You have no right to speak to my wife like that—"

"Your wife? She's no wife—"

He cut his mother short, his voice rarely raised now blistering with fury. "She is my wife, and I love her very much. If you have a problem with her, then you have a problem with me because Alysia is my heart. You speak to her like that again and I shall cut you off forever. Do you understand?"

Mrs. Pateras stared at her only child in shock, her mouth opening, eyes wide. And then she shook her head once, a slow, angry shake, before walking out of the bedroom and closing the door behind her.

Christos rolled up his shirtsleeves. "I'm sorry. I'm sorry she talked to you like that. I'm sorry I couldn't get back sooner."

Alysia stood rooted to the spot. She clutched the clothes tightly, too astonished, too overwhelmed to speak. The cashmere sweater tickled her neck, the long skirt rough against her bare arms. She could smell a whiff of her perfume on the sweater, a sweet light floral, a hint of Spring.

"You should have called me," he said, his features tight. "I left my numbers with my mother."

No point in telling him that his mother didn't share them. She swallowed, pressed the wadded clothes to her stomach. "Where were you?"

His dark gaze followed each jerky gesture, before lifting to her face, eyes searching hers. "I went to Paris."

She took an unsteady step to the chaise in the corner of the room and sank down. "Paris?"

"Then to London. I spoke with many people. People you worked for in Paris, the police there, and then on to Jeremy. He lives in London now. In a small dirty flat overlooking the Thames."

Jeremy alive, and well, Jeremy in a dirty flat near a river. But she didn't want to think of him, didn't want to be reminded of the grief they'd shared. Jeremy ruined her life once. She wouldn't let him ruin it again. "I don't want to talk about him."

"We have to."

"I can't, Christos, I can't. Please, not again. I told you everything—"

"No, not quite everything. You've forgotten the facts, Alysia, you've changed them."

She felt a tiny prick, almost like a beesting. "What do you mean?"

He moved across the room and sat down next to her on the chaise, drawing the bundled clothes from her arms. "It's time we talked about what really happened that afternoon in the apartment."

"I told you what happened."

"But that's not what happened. Look at me, Alysia. Look into my face." He waited until she dragged her gaze up, eyes meeting his. "The baby drowned," he said quietly, "but it's not your fault. You weren't even there. Somehow you've mixed the facts up, guilt and grief. You have to remember how it really happened, not the story you told me."

She couldn't speak, panic wrestling with hope and yet even as she dared to hope she remembered the truth. Alexi died, Alexi was dead, her baby, he was *her baby,* and it was *her fault.*

"Jeremy was the one watching him. You weren't home when Alexi drowned. You were painting—"

She struggled to rise but Christos caught her

around the waist, drawing her back down, onto his lap.

His arms circled her, holding her fast to his chest. "You loved your baby, my sweet Alysia. You loved that baby more than anyone could love a child and you didn't fail him."

"I should have been there. If I were there he wouldn't have drowned. I wouldn't have blinked, or moved a muscle. I wouldn't have turned my back, not for an instant, not for anything in this world!"

"I know. I know what a good mother you were. Your friends told me. Your neighbors told me. The police told me. That's what makes this such a tragedy. You did what you could—"

"It wasn't enough."

He stroked the back of her head, fingers detangling the long silky strands of hair. "Jeremy had been drinking. He claims he lost track of time."

"He drank too much," she whispered, awash in pain. It was awful, too awful to relive again and again and again. "He wasn't happy," she added dully, remembering his bitterness when he discovered that her father had cut her off, that there'd be no generous allowance, no financial support. He'd married her for her fortune and there'd been none.

"But were you?"

Her heart constricted. "I had my baby." She felt her throat close. "You see why I can't have children. And your mother is right. This marriage won't work. You must give the money back to my father. Find yourself a real bride."

"You are a real bride. You're my bride."

"But the dowry—"

"There was no dowry. Your father is bankrupt."

"Bankrupt?"

"I paid his debts, got rid of his creditors and set up a small nest egg in Switzerland for him. He needs something to live on."

Her mouth dropped open. "You mean, I have no inheritance? I've nothing?"

His lips twisted. "Nothing but me. I'm sorry, Alysia. I've been trying to figure out a way to break the news, but I didn't know how to tell you."

She felt a bubble of joy. This was actually wonderful news. She hated her father's money, had never wanted his money. Just his love. All she'd ever wanted from him was his love. "I don't suppose my father will give the money back to you," she said doubtfully.

"No, and I don't want it back, because I'm not about to give you up. I've waited for you for ten years. I first saw you over ten years ago in Athens, at a ship owners meeting. We were gathered in the living room and you interrupted the meeting to ask your father a question—"

"You were there?" she breathed.

His jaw thickened. "I hated what he did to you, I hated how he treated you. I vowed then and there to find you, to make you mine. I made a deal with your father, but it was for you, and me. I knew I could make you happy, and I will."

"How can you trust me after Alexi? Your mother, she hates me."

"I don't need her approval. I don't care what people think. I love you, and I want to be with you and that's all that matters."

"And there's really no inheritance."

"None. Zilch. You're as poor as a church mouse."

"That's too wonderful!" Tears filled her eyes, tears and a hint of laughter. For the first time in years she felt as though she could finally breathe. No inheritance, no pretense, no duty. Just love. And hope. "You really do love me?"

He stared deep into her eyes, his own dark depths full of emotion. "With all my heart and all my soul."

"Say it again."

"With all my heart, all my mind, all my body and all my soul. I was made for you, to love you, and only you." He kissed her then, stemming additional protests, silencing the intellect, letting emotion and sensation rule.

She woke the next morning nestled against him. It was early yet, not even six, and immediately her first thought was of Alexi, but instead of denying the flicker of pain, she drew a deep breath and said a prayer for him.

She did love him, she would always love him. As she finished her prayer Alysia felt a great wave of peace. The peace filled her, warm and light and bright, bringing tears to her eyes, but this time tears of happiness, and relief.

"Alysia?" Christos stirred, wrapped an arm

around her waist, drew her closer to him. "What's wrong?"

"I said a prayer for Alexi." Her voice broke. "But it's okay, I understand he's in God's hands, and I owe it to him to make my life matter, to make it better. I owe it to him to be strong."

"As long as you live, Alexi will live on, in your heart, and in your thoughts."

"Then I must live a good long life and never forget the blessings we've been given." She couldn't swallow around the lump in her throat, and burying her face in Christos's shoulder, her mouth pressed to his bare skin, she let go of the anger and the guilt and the shame.

She cried for those she'd loved and cried for those she'd lost. She even cried for the relationship she'd never had with her father.

Christos held her throughout. But at last, there were no more tears, and exhausted, she lifted her wet face. "I'm sorry," she sniffed, reaching for tissues. "That was rather appalling."

He kissed her brow, the tip of her nose, her tear-streaked mouth. "It's what you needed to do. Grieve. Love. Feel. Especially feel. You can't live all shut down. You're not a robot, you're a beautiful, smart, sensitive woman." He kissed her again, her lower lip quivering. "You can talk to me about Alexi as much as you want. And if you ever want to talk to someone else, you could do that, too. Whatever you want. Whatever you need."

She pressed her cheek to Christos's chest savoring the even beat of his heart. "You give me hope."

"Then believe, Alysia, believe we will have a wonderful life together, a new life that will be better than anything either of us have yet lived."

"Is it possible?"

"I know it is."

"How can you be so certain?"

"I just know, the same way I knew that day in Athens that I would find you again and make you mine. I was made to love you. And I shall. Always."

EPILOGUE

"CAREFUL! Watch out," Alysia called, jumping from the polished marble bench, shielding her eyes as she anxiously followed the toddler's progress down the flagstone path toward the fishpond.

"Gotcha." Christos laughed, swinging the wriggling little boy in the sailor jumper onto his shoulders. "I know where you were going."

"Fishies!" Two-year-old Nikos shouted, jabbing his father in the ear with a wet finger. "I wuv fishies."

Christos walked up the path, returning with the energetic toddler to the bench in the shade.

Alysia stood, arms outstretched to take the bouncing boy. Happily Nikos lunged into her arms, patting her face, kissing her cheek and then her mouth. "Mama."

Her heart turned over. "Yes, Mama loves you."

"Nikos wuvs fishies," he shouted, enthusiastically patting her face again.

"Careful with Mama," Christos said, reaching out to touch Nikos's small hand, gentling the tiny fingers.

"Mama," Nikos said again, kissing her cheek.

Alysia lifted her head, met Christos's dark gaze. "I'm fine," she whispered, even as the baby inside her moved. In just weeks there'd be another little Pateras running wild in the lovely rambling Colonial house.

Christos leaned down, placing a possessive kiss on her upturned lips. "You're so beautiful, especially now."

"You're blind."

"Not blind, just deeply in love." He kissed her again, over the top of Nikos's dark head. "How did we get so lucky?"

Her eyes burned and yet she smiled as tears welled up in her eyes, her heart brimming with happiness and love for Christos. It still staggered her, the joy she'd found with him. "I don't know. It's a miracle."

RED HOT REVENGE

There are times in a man's life...
When only seduction will settle old scores!

**Pick up our exciting new series
of revenge-filled romances—
they're recommened and red-hot!**

This month:
A SICILIAN SEDUCTION
by **Michelle Reid**
Harlequin Presents® #2175

Coming next month:
THE DETERMINED HUSBAND
by **Lee Wilkinson**
On-sale June 2001, Harlequin Presents® #2183

And look out for:
THE MARRIAGE DEMAND
by **Penny Jordan**
On-sale November 2001, Harlequin Presents® #2211

Available wherever Harlequin books are sold.

HARLEQUIN®
Makes any time special®

A brand-new story of
emotional soul-searching and family turmoil
by *New York Times* bestselling author

Penny Jordan

Featuring her famous
Crighton family!

STARTING OVER

Focusing on the elusive Nick Crighton and his
unexpected exploration of love, this richly woven story
revisits Penny Jordan's most mesmerizing family ever!

"Women everywhere will find pieces
of themselves in Jordan's characters."
—*Publishers Weekly*

Coming to stores in October 2001.

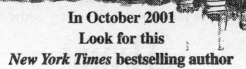

In October 2001
Look for this
New York Times bestselling author

BARBARA DELINSKY

in

Bronze Mystique

The only men in Sasha's life lived between the covers of her bestselling romances. She wrote about passionate, loving heroes, but no such man existed...til Doug Donohue rescued Sasha the night her motorcycle crashed.

AND award-winning Harlequin Intrigue author

GAYLE WILSON

in

Secrets in Silence

This fantastic 2-in-1 collection will be on sale October 2001.

HARLEQUIN®
Makes any time special®

Together for the first time
in one Collector's Edition!

New York Times bestselling authors

Barbara Delinsky

Catherine Coulter   Linda Howard

Forever Yours

A special trade-size volume containing three
complete novels that showcase the passion,
imagination and stunning power that these
talented authors are famous for.

Coming to your favorite retail outlet in December 2001.

HARLEQUIN®
Makes any time special®